Marian Womack is a bilingual Hispanic-British author, editor and translator of Weird fiction, horror, speculative fiction, and fiction of the Anthropocene. Her writing deals with man's relationship with nature and its loss through cross-genre, hybrid and experimental approaches, and she holds a PhD in Creative Writing and Environmental Humanities.

Marian's publications include the novels *The Swimmers* (2021), *The Golden Key* (2020), and *On The Nature of Magic* (2023). Her short fiction has been included in numerous collaborative works, used in art installations, and collected in the volumes *Lost Objects* (2018), and *Out of the Window, Into the Dark* (2024). She co-edited, with Gary Budden, the international eco-fiction anthology *An Invite to Eternity: Tales of Nature Disrupted* (2019), and is a contributor to *Writing the Future: Essays on Crafting Science Fiction* (2023). She has taught creative writing, publishing studies and book history in Spain and the UK, and is the first Spanish graduate of the Clarion Writer's Workshop.

Marian's work has been included in year's best's anthologies and lists, and shortlisted for British Fantasy Awards and British Science Fiction Association Awards. She is a member of the Climate Fiction Writer's League.

manner that I suspect we will come to recognise as uniquely Womack.'

Laura Mauro, Black Static

'Addresses humankind's senseless despoliation of its home in subtle, profoundly affecting ways.'

Timothy J. Jarvis, Los Angeles Review of Books

'Incredibly powerful.'

Charles Payseur

'A beautiful, haunting eulogy to our planet.'

Eco-Fiction

LOST OBJECTS

MARIAN WOMACK

CALQUE PRESS

This collection was previously published by Luna Press Publishing (Edinburgh, 2018). All stories have been revised for this edition, and in some cases changes made.

Cover design © Vince Haig 2024
Edited and Typeset by Calque Press
http://calquepress.com
ISBN: 978-1-9162321-9-8
Type: Hoefler Text
British Library Cataloguing-in-Publication Data
A catalogue record for this book is available from the British Library
Calque Press
An Imprint of Nevsky Editions Ltd.
2024

Contents

Introduction

There are books for when you're bored. Plenty of them. There are books for when you're calm. The best kind, in my opinion. There are also books for when you're sad. And there are books for when you're happy. There are books for when you're thirsty for knowledge. And there are books for when you're desperate.

Roberto Bolaño, painted on the wall in Desperate Literature Bookshop, Madrid, Spain

I first heard of Marian Womack in 2021 from my Spanish friend Sofia Barker, while I was visiting Madrid. We were in Desperate Literature, a marvellous bookshop that sells work in Spanish and English. Like Sofia, they were huge advocates for Marian's writing.

I remembered the name, so bought *Lost Objects* when I saw that it had been shortlisted for a British Fantasy Award in both the Best Collection *and* Best Newcomer category, and that "Kingfisher", one of the stories in the volume, had been nominated for a British Science Fiction Association Award.

Lost Objects is a slim volume that belies the weight of its subject matter—ecological devastation, extinction, evolution and bioengineering. Marian Womack records the trajectory of our malign influence on the planet without flinching.

Marian uses science fiction, horror, fairy tales, the weird and even alternative history in pursuit of her goals. Her stories have a dreamlike quality, almost hallucinatory in places. She depicts a world that is recognisable but that has been forced to evolve, and which remembers its former self, be it in Andalusia, Norfolk or on a Scottish island.

What makes her writing both direct and vital is that it's underpinned by small details of domestic life described in beautiful prose. The losses she records are deeply personal ones, intrinsically bound to global devastation, which makes the unimaginable wholly intimate and immediate.

If *Lost Objects* is a dream of the near future, then we are sleepwalking towards our fate. As I write this our planet is subject to droughts, flooding and loss of species. We are embroiled in wars and political meltdown. Have we always been on the brink of catastrophe, or is it just that now we're more aware of it? I feel like we've passed the tipping point of redemption. The world is in a desperate state and, as such, *Lost Objects* is a book for desperate times.

Priya Sharma
Wirral, UK, 2024

LOST OBJECTS

I

ORANGE DOGS

Sie warnen vor Giftigkeit[*]

LOOKING THROUGH THE THRESHOLD OF THE FRONT room, his wife's bedroom now, he caught a glimpse of her gigantic silhouette. The swollen pregnant belly seemed about to explode. The mountain of flesh, hidden under a knitted bedspread, lifted and sank, lifted and sank, to the faltering rhythm of her breathing.

He put the kettle on and ran upstairs. He took his time shaving, allowing the blade to flick water at the mirror with a dull spatter. He rinsed it and towelled his face dry before heading downstairs; the kettle was whistling. In the kitchen, the stagnant air of last night's work met him, heavy and sickly-sweet.

[*] *They warn that they are poisonous*, from a German treatise on butterflies.

On the counter sat the fruits of his labours: six jars of shining golden marmalade. He held one of them up to the light. It did not move. The liquid had set. He allowed himself a slight smile of relief.

After cutting two slices of bread and rubbing them with tarragon, he breakfasted standing up, sipping at his hot tea. It was the day of the barter market, or rather the day the militia turned a blind eye to non-official transactions, which was the same thing. He looked at the marmalade and ate hurriedly, worrying that he'd miss the best offers.

He liked getting to the market when they were still setting up the stalls, putting together planks and wooden boxes protected by rusty metal frames and oilcloth. He would look at everything. Only then would he decide where to trade, and with whom.

The map on the kitchen wall was a stain of purples and reds, drawn on top of the furrows of the canal system and the river. The river was a curve that surrounded the city from the north, squeezed it, hugged it like a drowning lover. The river was the danger. The purple patches showed the areas that had been flooded in the last two years; the red dots marked possible danger zones. He felt a stab of pain in his chest, but this was now a more diffuse hurt, not like the sharp needle of months back.

It was with a mixture of apprehension and defiance that he had started to study the river. Grief for what had happened with his wife's last pregnancy, alongside a furious certainty that he would not let it happen again. He forced himself to take another sip of tea, which burnt his tongue and tasted mouldy. The most important thing was to continue with those small gestures, the little familiar things. Shave every morning. Sip a comforting cup of something resembling tea.

The noise from the back garden took him to the window. He allowed himself to imagine fox cubs, leverets. He hadn't seen any for ages. But neither had he lost hope that they would reappear, and he continued greasing and recalibrating the traps he had set several months ago.

The garden was a muddy square, abandoned and haggard. Guilt squeezed his chest again. He couldn't do anything about this, not yet. His wife had looked after the garden. That's how it had always been.

What he saw was a woman bent over a sort of gigantic bramble of aromatic herbs, grown up all by itself after the garden had been left to rot. She was wearing a brown cotton tunic and army boots, her hair dyed blue. Several amulets were clinking round her neck, little jars of cures for almost all illnesses. The woman stood up slowly, sniffed at the herbs she had just gathered and turned to walk towards the back door. She entered the kitchen and directed her steps to where the kettle still was steaming.

'Good morning.'

'Good morning.'

The woman moved round the room as if she were walking round her own house. Without hesitating, she opened the little cupboard where the cups and saucers and teapots were kept, washed the herbs at the sink, smashed them into a one-person teapot and poured hot water on top of them.

He watched her without saying anything.

The doula had been with them for almost four months, during which time he had been able to go to work every morning feeling the pain in his chest relax a little.

'It's the barter market today,' the doula said.

'That's right. And I need to pay you for the week.'

He held a jar of marmalade out to the woman. She frowned.

'Is that real marmalade?'

'Yes.'

'From real oranges?'

The man nodded.

'It's not synthetic?'

'Can't you smell it?' he said, waving vaguely at the air in the kitchen. The doula shrugged.

'I don't remember how anything smells any more.'

He couldn't stop his lip curling up a little. The doula was still young, childbearing age. He felt a guilty pang all of a sudden and composed his face. The woman accepted the jar, still disbelieving.

'This would be enough for the whole month.'

'It's for a week.'

'But...'

'I insist.'

The woman stroked the jar.

'In the black market...'

'I'm going to be late,' he said.

Before he left the house, he went through into the front bedroom.

———

It took ten minutes by bicycle to reach the market square. He had to add in five more for the morning river inspection. He decided to push himself, to get this time down to thirteen or even twelve minutes. He took Ferry Path at full speed and came up onto the Fort St George, stopping in the middle of the small bridge. The bicycle halted with a slight jingle from the jars of marmalade in the wooden box on the back.

What came down the river was a vague brown stain of liquid mud, which brought to mind the thick blood of an enormous animal. The opaque water led to only one conclusion: the river was rising. He took a deep breath, considering the dark current that pushed the river onwards.

It would be impossible to imagine another outcome than the eventual flooding; he knew the signs. The mud-lie water was punctuated by rubbish, stems and stalks, branches, trash, clothes, cardboard—all from who knows where—that floated on the bright oily surface, showing where the accursed water was flowing and how fast.

If he shut his eyes he could still see the bundle of stained towels falling from that same railing a year ago; he could even hear the phantom cry of a newborn baby. He forced his mind to compose a different image: at the last moment the child had taken flight, had headed up to a clean blue sky.

The cold snapped him back to reality: a sky filled with storm clouds, eternally tainted as a blackboard, bruised and sick, hanging over them like a stone, air so thin and cruel it had turned everything into a lifeless swamp.

—•—

After leaving his bicycle in the patch that served as a parking lot he crossed the deserted street in the direction of the market. The proceedings were only just coming to life. He went past the stalls, looking at the goods still packed in their boxes, the pedal-powered carts, the eel-baskets. He rummaged among the bicycle spare parts, and the woollens, all in that characteristic indeterminate drab colour that years of use had given them. He noticed sadly that there was hardly any food. Almost no one traded the food from their own gardens any more.

A group at one of the corner posts excited his curiosity. The larger the number of customers, the more likely it was that there would be something to eat. His instinct was right. They were selling eatables. At a distance he could see ducks and coots hanging from a rope, covered in tar to preserve them. He made his way through the crush until he got to the side of an old man who was staring open-mouthed at the goods on offer. He stood stock still, and almost dropped the box with the jars of marmalade.

In a large metal washtub, the stallholder had five or six giant swallowtail butterflies, huge and tarnished yellow-brown, each with a blue eye on its wing, unusual spots for this species, or at least that's how it appeared to his expert gaze. He calculated that each butterfly must measure more than twenty inches across. And they were fresh, no doubt about that. Fresh but frayed. The bottom of the washtub was a muddy pit of water and earth and the remains of those bright wings, ruined by death and by the hunt. Those broken wings were beautiful: the deep blue eyespots, which seemed to be staring straight at him, were nothing more than a chance discrepancy, but they almost provoked the old familiar pain in the pit of his stomach, mixed with some other emotion he did not recognise.

'Orange dogs! Orange dogs! Ducks, coots!' cried the stallholder.

'Where did you get them?' he found himself asking. There had not been butterflies like these for several years: he had only seen dissected specimens.

'They're not mine, I didn't catch them. I'm only selling.'

'It's very important that you tell me. I need to know,' he insisted. The man lifted his hands in a gesture of surrender.

'Mate... I only sell them. I don't know anything else.'

He managed to convince himself that his interest had been purely professional, and he walked away from the stall, from time to time turning back to look at it, as if he still couldn't quite believe what he had just seen. The old man he had been standing next to followed him with his eyes.

———

The morning went by much as expected. In exchange for his jars he got supplies and parts to fix the door of the wood-burning stove in his kitchen. But the biggest prize was the medical supplies that the preserves had managed to win him. When he only had one jar left, the old man came up to him.

'Excuse me... Is that real marmalade?'

'Yes,' he muttered. He was exhausted, and only wanted to leave. His eyes kept on wandering to the insect stall. 'Do you want to make a trade?'

'I haven't seen marmalade since I was a kid, much less eaten it. May I ask how...?'

'I work in the Old University Natural History Museum. We have a pass to go to London twice a year, to the National Museum.' He didn't normally explain so much about his life, but he only wanted the old man to shut up. 'Do you want to trade or don't you?'

The man's face clouded over. His little eyes were the only things that still shone, reflecting this liquid gold.

'I don't have anything.'

'Goodbye, then.'

But as he was turning to go, the old man said: 'The only thing I can offer you is information, perhaps something you want to hear.'

Had he heard right? Information? Who was this man, and what did he know about him? What did he know about his wife and his dead son?

'What the hell are you trying to say?'

'The butterflies...'

Everything clicked.

'I know where they've got a nest.'

The old man was trying to string him along, for sure.

'Listen, my job is studying the *Papilionidae*... I know they don't live in nests. So you can get lost.'

'These ones do,' the old man said.

He realised that he was, in fact, intrigued.

'All right. Okay. I'll give you my last jar in exchange for whatever it is you want to tell me.'

The old man smiled like a child.

'But I must warn you that if you're lying to me then I'll denounce you to the militia. I am a third rank specialist worker, and they will listen to me.'

This was just a bluff. His rank had been no use at all when his wife needed medical assistance. He knew they wouldn't have even deigned to come and pick up his son's body after the child had been stillborn in the sixth month, so he didn't know if what he was saying was true or not. But the old man seemed to believe him. They walked off to an alleyway and made their exchange, a fairly common exchange, all in all: information for food.

———

He cycled furiously. In the early dusk, the water was as dark as the sky, and shone with spectral glints.

After a time he realised the impossibility. The disused lock the old man had spoken of was several miles away, and night was falling. He would have to try again tomorrow.

He turned round and went home, following the river, which kept twisting and twisting, and he was incapable of making himself look to see if the water had covered the greenish marks of its last high point.

———

After his careful additions, the map looked the next morning like a grotesque purple and red stain.

If his predictions were correct, then the floods could be worse than in previous years. He wondered if anyone else had spent the last few months watching the water, making calculations on a plan of the town. It was clear that the authorities had not foreseen the consequences of a possible new rise in the water level. There had been no official announcements or advice about what to do in that case; the people were once again abandoned to their fate.

He spent the first part of the morning examining the map. Bates Lock was quite a long way for him to go and come back after work. It was not uncommon for night to come upon him while he was in the museum, cataloguing specimens or inspecting exhibits.

Just as he was about to leave, the doula asked to speak to him.

'You have to be ready,' she said. 'It could be any day now.'

He looked straight at her for a few seconds; he wanted to thank her. To tell her that they wouldn't be where they were without her. But he froze. His tongue felt dry and scratchy inside his mouth.

'Thank you,' he managed after the woman had already left the kitchen.

He left the house and got onto his bicycle, but he did not start pedalling. Something stopped him. His mind was a blank. He couldn't think about anything, couldn't decide anything.

Bates Lock floated in his head.

Then he had an idea. He would ask one of his neighbours' children to come over the bridge into the centre of town to find him if anything happened, *if she went into labour*, he forced himself to think, strangely aware of the meaning of the words. Only then was he ready to go.

———

While crossing the Fort St George Bridge he went over in his mind the route to the lock that he had memorised. He did so compulsively, trying to push aside his fear of that thing, the other thing, that was about to happen. In the leaden sky a flock of geese circled, a ragged "V" with no apparent direction, stunted and lost, spiralling in its vague escape to nowhere.

He reached the museum in less than twenty minutes, his best time yet. Thanks to his job there he had not lost his house, and had even managed to garner certain privileges: some food, warmth during the winter, access to certain books. The biannual trips to the capital. Who knew how, but it was a place where strange food managed to appear, memories of a memory, things whose taste and smell no one remembered clearly.

The group he was working for was trying to throw a little light on the reasons why, after their appearance on the island formerly known as England, the *papilio cresphontes* had developed certain unusual habits, some of them violent—for example the males eating the females, and occasionally even the larvae. This had been a key to the early disappearance of the insects. Some of them had developed a strange venom, and it was believed that the unusual colours in the eyespots was a warning of its presence. Shortly after their appearance they had given themselves over to hunting smaller creatures, such as field mice, and even on occasion baby hares, flying away with their prey immobilised.

These were no more than hypotheses. After the irreplaceable loss of most of the books, of the computer communication system, of the telephones, of almost everything that had provided information and facilitated scientific exchange, they knew almost nothing. They had to start again from the beginning, to examine this new world. This was their duty, the important job survivors like him had to carry out.

His access to books was very limited, but he knew German, and most surviving treatises on butterflies were in this language. He only knew how to operate a small number of the heavy brass instruments, to turn the crank and adjust the microscope lenses, to fill the little stoves with coal and wood, to filter the water for the distillations. His job was important but not irreplaceable. But he felt it was his duty to find the lock. It was vitally important, if a small population of *Papilionidae* had established itself in the county, that they had access to it. If the nest was there, he would share his findings with his colleagues.

The *papilio cresphontes*—commonly called 'orange dogs'—had disappeared in the same sudden fashion that they had appeared in the records. The annals recorded their arrival as being after the first great flood. A large part of the town had been submerged. The canals where the students had punted, with their straw hats and their picnic baskets, their books of poetry or mathematics, had overflowed. The colleges of the university bore the brunt of the furious water which finished off the destruction of all their treasures, a destruction that had been started by the months-long freeze, unexpected and murderous, which had preceded the waters. The world's most expensive wines were drowned in the college cellars, and the large kitchens and dining rooms and studies lost their impressive beauty under the force of the silt. Whole libraries of incunabulae were lost. The whole town was flooded: Jesus Green, Mill Lane, the Backs, like a less luminous Venice in its death throes.

But the water was not exactly hell; that was still to come. For after the flood had come the summer, the long-awaited summer. The first of the hottest summers ever recorded. Fifteen fateful years of suffocating heat, damp, mosquitoes, monstrous and terrifying greenery. The flood had surpassed all expectations, but in the end the water had been sucked up in some form by the earth, risen in order to fall back down again, drop by drop, only to be spat out and multiplied in the form of a swampish miasma under the survivors' feet, after which the ground had exploded into an impossible jungle where all kinds of unknown flora had sprung into life, bringing the strange fauna along with it. The town had transformed itself into the unexpected home of parrots and parakeets, the river the cradle for swarms of mosquitoes so dense that they sometimes covered whole houses.

And then came the giant insects, like dark angels who had climbed up from hell by mistake. The centipedes, the caterpillars, the moths and the butterflies, huge and ugly, brightly coloured, pot-bellied. The forms and shapes of the eyespots on their wings were not recognisable as those of any catalogued species.

That late and lengthy summer had not been a period of truce for the exhausted human race. Even after the waters went down there was less to eat. The unexpected heat led to old diseases, which had been cured generations ago, returned now to decimate the population.

And then came the eternal autumn, in which he had been born. They ploughed the fields once more, they reverted to the old wisdoms. But it was too late, many people thought.

The butterflies disappeared then almost entirely; the caterpillars buried themselves in the earth so as never to come out again.

———

He had been bluffing with the old man. The sanitation patrols never came round now, not even to register a death. They only let themselves be seen, descending from their bumblebee helicopters in masks and white jumpsuits, when there was a suspicion of cannibalism. This was something that they were determined to stamp out root and branch, vanishing suspects with them up into the sky. No one came when his wife went into early labour. Not even the doula could cross the river to help them, because that year it had risen more than ever.

It had been his fault as well. He knew that much.

He had not paid attention to the signs.

The sunflower field, the one he could see in the distance from his office at the museum, completely submerged, the heads of the flowers the only visible things above the grey water. The coots walking into the middle of Jesus Green, leaving their watery nests, making themselves easy to catch.

He did not want to think about his guilt. But she had not abandoned the garden, had carried potatoes and parsnips, her belly sticking out, proud of the activity she could still perform. That's how she had been until almost the sixth month, until the day she started to bleed.

He had to help with the birth himself, to carry out that horrendous task. The river had broken its banks as well, had flooded Jesus Green, had flooded Midsummer Common, had almost reached his house. His wife had not stopped bleeding until the doula arrived, but she had survived. A miracle. If he had helped stop her haemorrhage then he had no recollection of how he had done so. The baby had not been so lucky. He remembered it as a liquid mass of unmoving flesh and blood. The doula had told him that it would not survive, that he should bury the bundle before the mother woke up. Had she said he was dead? He simply was not sure.

Recently he had started to remember those horrid hours differently, seeing the child's eyes in his mind; a cruel joke of his exhausted brain, for the little thing never opened them. He could still feel the little chilled body, the doula insisting that he bury it in the garden, almost opening the back door and pushing him into the inhospitable outside. He stood there for a while, a bundle of bloody towels in his hands, and started to walk somewhere.

Those memories might have been invented, tainted by the shadowy twilight that hung above them, or by the thick fog that rolled up often from the river, conquering the world. It was easy to call up strange memories when the fog came upon you at the riverside; it was easy to get disoriented. Everything, his memories and his daily life, seemed changed by that shadowy unreality.

He decided to go home. He could not allow it to happen again. *It would not happen again.* By now he understood the signs better, and realised that the city would flood again in a few hours. He could see lightning far away, a vast electrical storm, oddly silent in the distance, and realised that this was the last warning, that soon after the storm reached them and burnt itself out, everything would once again be covered under the stain of black water.

The birth happened that afternoon, and it was much quicker than the one a year earlier. A few hours of pain, and then everything seemed to take place in ten minutes: a few pushes, the doula shouting instructions and cheering her along, and soon he was holding in his arms a boy, purple with the effort of the labour, long and apparently fully formed, alive.

That night he stole a couple of hours of sleep away from his constant fear. His dreams were troubled, filled with water. The baby had little electric blue eyes. *It's too soon to tell,* the dream-doula said, *but he looks like he'll have his mother's eyes.*

In the dream his wife died, and he sat up for her wake, feeling lost and alone.

He woke up with his heart filled with grief into the comfort of the real world, realising that everything was fine, that they both were fine.

His dream had been very different. He had been aware that she was dead because of the way her face had changed, becoming dry and powdery as parchment. People who died only needed a few hours to gain this uncertain texture of fragility in their skin, flaky and falling back against their bones.

There was a moment when he felt a new tremor run through his soul.

He went to the front room and entered without making any noise, to lean over his wife. Her skin was glowing, and the child's was as well, and both of them were moving slowly to the deliberate rhythm of their breathing.

It was then that he knew, as sudden as a flash of lightening. The bundle of rugs, blood, and flesh, that was his son a year ago had not dried out either; his skin had not become the parchment-like texture.

This was a fact; at last he had found one.

He sat at the foot of the bed for a few moments, and cried in silence.

It took him all his strength of will to go out without making any noise, shutting the front door carefully. The sky was an endless black stain. The canals spread out before him, apparently endless. When he reached the lock he would not have been able to say how long he had been riding for, or how long it had been since he left his wife and son in the distant town.

The light after the storm spilled ghostly onto the canal. The lock was closed, abandoned. The sign that said 'No Bathing Allowed' still hung on one of the walls of the lockkeeper's hut, its red letters bleeding rust and mould. On the horizon a late bolt of lightning shone out. A few distant groans and the unexpected howl of some living creature broke through to reality.

He would not have been able to bury the bundle that afternoon, just a year ago, a brief dozen months, which he remembered as distant as if it had taken place a decade back.

No, he not buried it, contradicting the doula's instructions. What had happened was different: night had fallen when he found that his footsteps had taken him to the Fort St George Bridge. He watched the river for a while as it nearly rubbed against the metal structure, even after going down for a day. The water seemed as dark to him as the sky. He balanced the bundle against the rails, and just when he decided that he was going to go home to bury it, the bundle slipped from his trembling hands. And then he thought he heard the child make some kind of sound, no doubt another sick joke on the part of his mind; this was too cruel to be true. Whatever had happened, it was now too late, as the bundle sank with a dull noise.

Looking down he saw nothing. He went to the other side, following the current, but didn't see the bundle pass under the bridge. It must have gone into the deepest part of the water.

Just then he saw that winged creature flying up, carrying something whitish and stained. What the creature then let drop from the sky were his towels, and in the uncertain twilight he could have sworn that it was a gigantic butterfly, one that had not been seen for years, flying ochre and leaden into the dusk, carrying his dead unshrouded son like the spoil of a monstrous bird of prey.

———

He considered the lock—a rectangle filled up almost halfway with stagnant water, with all kinds of natural and artificial rubbish floating on top.

He thought it must be deceptively easy to drown in a lock.

There was no doubt that he was in the right place. He could hear clearly a *papilio*'s wings moving. But he couldn't see where the creature was. He cranked his lantern's handle, which would maintain the light for the time being. That's when he saw it—a square hole, artificially made to repair some of the lock's mechanism. He threw himself into the water.

It was only then that he understood how dirty the water was. His arms and his head got instantly covered in a dark oily liquid, whatever it was that the water had transformed itself into over the decades, stock still like a dead sea. He did not waste much time in thinking. He pushed his way through the tins and the beams and the branches and reached the spot where the square hole was; he held on with both hands and lifted himself up. He managed to get half his body in, only his legs still hanging out.

He heard the murmur—birds, bats? Butterflies. *Papilios*. Orange dogs. All of them with the same unusual electric blue stains in the wings, so similar to his wife's wide open eyes as she pushed and pushed to let their child into the world.

Nothing there, of course. He thought he could hear a child whimpering at the end of a large tunnel, and tried to crawl towards the sound. But he could not move. Then the butterfly came out in his direction.

The largest one he had ever seen.

Obviously not a child. Nothing human could moan like that. This made him relax a little. What exactly was he looking for there? What had he hoped to find? His overwrought mind could only hint at the reply to that question.

Another noise broke upon him—the unmistakeable and deafening racket of furious water. The lock would soon flood, killing off those creatures. Killing him as well, if he did not get moving. He chose life, surprising even himself.

Once again he came out to the stagnant water. He looked for the steps cut into the stone, intended to help anyone climb up the canal's artificial bank, but he slipped and sank. Water filled his lungs. He tasted it avidly as the water soaked into him. This was the end. With a superhuman effort, he moved his arms and found himself beating against the wall. This time he climbed the steps on fingertips, clawing the life out of the stone itself. Without knowing how, he managed to give himself a push and got a foot onto the bottom step. Climbing up was easier than he had thought. He found himself next to the canal, sprawled on the ground, covered in dark mud and spitting out the black water which he had found so sweet a minute ago. He tried to sit up then, but something pushed him back, making him bite the earth. He turned over.

Then he saw them. Spat out of the hole. A swarm of *papilios* that went following their queen, escaping from whatever it was that had made them grow in such a supernatural way, escaping from the rising waters that would soon have drowned them.

He got on his bicycle and pedalled away as quickly as he could, more quickly than he had ever pedalled before in his life, in the opposite direction, against the current, back to his wife, back to his newborn son, back home.

LITTLE RED DROPS

I.

WHEN SHE WOKE UP THE WOMEN ASKED WHO SHE WAS and how she had got to their part of the world. She told them a fiction: backpacking, hitching a ride, a broken-down truck. The driver's idea that she would sleep in the old people's commune.

The little houses broke forth like mirages, white shadows, their corners lost in the soft wall of the falling snow. She cleaned the steam off the window with her hand, and the gloves she had worn while she slept got wet. Then she looked through the glass: a back yard with rubbish bins, bits of plastic, piles of bricks, uralite panels, what was left of an improvised and abandoned construction site. Yellowish reflections that shaped agonising shadows over the morning; and her, looking out over the dull silence.

She found a house. Abandoned buildings multiplied in the area, and the daughter of one of the old ladies agreed to rent her one. They went there in an old car, directly imported from the previous era. A different world, so distant and yet so close. The price was three hundred dollars per month, a small fortune. They went in. The house had a wooden floor, a good-size stove opposite the main door, an old television set. It was cold inside, with that peculiar smell that reminded her of her grandmother: a sick sweetness, boiled cabbage, piles of newspapers.

'You shouldn't go near the forest,' the woman said. 'It can be dangerous. Especially at night.'

She spoke while opening windows, rearranging cushions with bursting energy, and in a second she had lit a fire. She unpacked the groceries they had bought from red-and-white-lined plastic bags. Olga saw a teapot, enough casseroles to cook for a large family, dark brown dishes and glasses, colourful rugs nailed to the walls. A statue of the Virgin in a corner of the room, surrounded by the bright wax of burnt-out candles.

'There's a train that comes on Thursdays and stops at the station. It sells vegetables and other little things.' They had seen the station from the car. It was a plank of dark wood in the middle of the forest, broken in two by the black line of the rails. 'There is also a shop, but it doesn't open every day.'

'I'll be fine.'

The other woman closed her red jacket, put her hood up and started looking at the tips of her shoes. A wettish snow was picking up, making the road look dirty. The silence didn't last long. Olga took her money out of her pocket, counted three hundred of the only currency accepted worldwide, and handed it over.

'I'll call you in a couple of days to check that everything is okay.'

Olga didn't reply, surprised to hear that there was a phone, that it was still connected.

The first thing she did when she was alone was switch on the television. It still ran on autopilot, old programmes broadcast from who knew where on a loop. A wolf was running after a riding hood in mini-skirt and fake breasts. She was so cold she put her coat back on. Soon the heating would be running though the hidden arteries of the little house, and it would be warm and cosy. She had been instructed never to let the stove go out; she would find wood enough at the back of the house piled for that purpose.

She put the kettle on and filled the teapot. Something moved inside; there was nothing, only the darkened herbs left behind a century ago, as black as insects. She threw them out with a firm shake of her hand.

She walked to the window and looked out. The snow is not silent, she thought. It had its own music, its own voice, calling her tirelessly.

Was it then that she saw her, the little girl in the hoodie? It was difficult to know; she had seen nothing really. There was nobody there. Only a parked car in the next hut, a dilapidated well in the middle of the empty yard, pine trees, rubbish bins in subdued colours. The snow had confused her. There can be mirages in the snow. She'd read about it online.

I've got here! she thought, excited for no particular reason. Nothing had happened yet. But it was one of those places where time seemed to stop, and there was nowhere to go and nothing to do. All those were good things.

I'll be whole again, she thought. I'll be more like myself, more like I used to be. I'll be whole again, once I've done it. For him, she did not waste one thought.

2.

Don't tell them, her friend had said. Let them think you have got there by chance, or the Nana won't help you.

She found her, inhabiting a makeshift shack at the entrance to a little cave, an island made of wood, metal and tin, scraps of other people's lives. Up the ridges on that side of the valley, the loneliness was unbearable. It was a no-man's land. The white sierra in the distance, the pine copses, cut in half by the train line. Now and again, the ruin of a little dwelling was visible, or perhaps a farm. They were longish one-storey buildings, crawling over the slopes like faded reptiles. Their windows were closed and shut like dead eyes. They were home to bats and feral cats, those abandoned places, half-built because the money to put them up had run out. Or because someone had died, or disappeared. A ruined space, where whatever was meant to happen had already passed them by.

The Nana was holding a cigarette in her callused hands.

'Yes? What is it? What do you want, child?'

Olga stood on the threshold to her self-made home. The woman had crossed herself when she saw her.

'Just to get my fortune told.'

The old woman shrugged, ill-humouredly.

'I don't perform such tricks! Go away!'

'Oh, but I know you do.' She took a bunch of dollars from her pocket. The Nana looked at it and crossed herself once more. She didn't take the money, but invited her in.

She could imagine her there, day in and day out, with those oversized male boots, going out into the early cold to feed the chickens and rabbits. From the half-opened door she could see the improvised cages with their little furry things, hear the cracking laughter of the birds.

She was invited to sit, and to drink tea out of an old teapot, where the leaves were changed after who knows how long. The Nana stubbed out her cigarette, only to light up again at once. She was telling the truth, of course. She possessed no Tarot cards, but Olga had not come exactly for that reason. She was looking to get something else done, something very precise indeed.

They talked for a while. And then the old lady blurted, out of nowhere:

'Your mother. She was special. All her virtues...'

The oddness of the little speech hung there, in midair, and neither of the women knew what to do with it for a moment. But an answer was required to this portent.

'Which virtues?'

'She would never try to do what you are trying to do. She would have never asked what you have come here looking for.'

So she knew.

Olga was asked to produce a photograph. She did. Olga was told that a life would be taken. No other way to do this than with little red drops of fresh blood. She paid for the small animal that would be slaughtered.

'Those things that happen to you, child, you invite them in. You are more wolf than sheep!' The Nana crossed herself rapidly, twice.

'Okay...' Olga managed to utter, unsure of where the conversation was going.

They drunk from their cups and the old lady laughed, revealing holes in her cheeks.

46

Later, they went out into the yard. Olga looked on, half fascinated and half disgusted. The woman held the rabbit by its ears and slowly introduced the knife into its neck. It was a delicate, soft movement. Two little dogs appeared out of nowhere and started barking excitedly around her. After that, she took out the knife and let the rabbit bleed out slowly, slowly, while the little creature shook with all its might. In that way, she explained, its meat was tenderer.

Olga had not known the meat would be consumed. She hoped it didn't need to be by her. The rabbit disgusted her; it made her think of a large rat.

The Nana bound the animal's corpse tight in newspapers, and held it over.

'Here,' she said.

'I don't want it.'

'Suit yourself,' she spat, and left the bundle on her kitchen table. Olga inspected the ancient face, trying to read there if she was at last free from her unrequited love. It was a curiously serene face, as if the woman were now resting after a huge effort of will.

'Will it work?' she asked.

'Will what work?'

'The cure, if I don't eat the rabbit.'

'I have no idea what you are talking about, child.'

Olga didn't know what to say. Perhaps she had come to the wrong place after all.

'Take this as well,' the Nana said when she was ready to leave, offering her a piece of Easter bun. 'With the compliments for the season.'

'I do not want it, but thank you.'

'Take it,' the old lady insisted. 'A little bread so you can't get lost.'

And she did take it, feeling it was important.

3.

She put on her coat and went round the back of the house. Shit. Fuck. Her landlady had said there would be enough wood for several weeks. She could imagine what had happened. There were only old ladies left there, old ladies in their old dachas, lonely lives in the middle of nowhere. A village of three streets, populated by old women. Old women who had taken her wood.

Shit. Fuck.

A piece of bright colour sticking out in the white. Olga approached and kicked it. It was a plastic boat, a child's toy. The snow absorbs everything, like the sea does, and like the sea it spits out only the corpses. How strange it all was, this brave new white world.

She walked back to the front of the house and found that someone was waiting for her.

'Good morning.' A young man with a dog, coming out of the forest, his arms filled with branches.

'Good morning.'

'I'm your neighbour. We share the well.'

'Hi, I'm renting the house.'

They shook hands without exchanging names.

'Listen... do you want some of this? I've noticed you're running short.'

She was thankful for the offer, and they went in. He gave her all the wood he was carrying, and she offered him some tea. They sipped it eating butter biscuits, past their due date.

She hated this, accepting the help of a man; but she had to.

He sat in front of the fire, stretching his legs as if he were a regular visitor. The dog was lying at his feet, next to the fire but keeping contact with his owner.

'Do you want to go to the copse now?'

It was an odd question.

'What for?'

'I can show you how to find wood. It's easy.'

She understood.

'I've been told it is dangerous to enter into the forest.'

He laughed.

'That's not a forest! It's too small. We would have to walk it for a long time to find a place dense enough to be called a forest.'

'Well, I've been told...'

'I see. Yes, it's better not to go in. Sometimes there are boys from town. They come here to drink. They are always looking for things to steal. They

come at night. Some of them walk into the snow...
They die there sometimes. Not used to it.'

'In the forest?'

'They fall asleep, or get lost there and never come
out.'

She said nothing.

'Yes, those boys can be dangerous sometimes.'

It seemed to her that the snowed-in forest
sounded a hundred times more deadly.

She accompanied him to the door. She didn't
want him to go, or to stay.

'I'll see you around.'

She smiled, unsure how to answer.

4.

It was still difficult to assimilate the strength the
new status quo demanded.

In the mornings she forced herself to go out,
and went through the three streets of the village.
There were frozen trees, the smell of burning
wood, an unexpected group of children playing
with a plastic ball or running after each other over
the frozen river.

She saw him sometimes, with his dog.
Sometimes he brought her more wood, or water
from the well equidistant between their two little
houses, that dishevelled construction that had at
first seemed abandoned to Olga, a useless pile of

rocks, dirty with moss in the middle of the yard. And once the snow settled in it turned out to be their only source of drinking water: brownish water, with a faint taste of mould. She knew she ought to be thankful for it.

She soon got the hang of keeping the stove constantly refilled with wood that she had previously dried in the oven. Inside it, in a little alcove designed for some other purpose, she kept a continuous provision of baked potatoes. In that eternal renewing of the potatoes, of the wood, the fire, the water that became her tea, her shallow baths, there boiled an activity that settled the rhythm of the freakish winter.

She waited. That was all she had to do. And it was as good a place to wait as any other.

It won't happen immediately, her friend had explained. Wait for the call, the letter. But he will disappear. A life for a life. Little red drops. She saw them sometimes in her dream, floating before her eyes.

One morning she went to the window and saw her neighbour by the well, filling plastic containers for both houses. He was courteous, and persistent in his courtesies. And she would have to give in sometime.

She saw that he wasn't alone. The steam in the window resolved itself into an unknown face, which looked back in her direction. And what she had thought was a dog turned out to be a child, a girl of some nine years old, ten perhaps, standing next to him. She was very straight, very still, very pale.

She came out, but as soon as she opened the door she saw that there was no one there with him, only the dog. Next to the well she could see some little drops of red, so oddly there, put in the middle of the white with no source to account for them.

'Hi!'

'Hi... Listen, who was that girl?'

'Which girl?'

Had she really expected a different answer?

'A child, really. She was standing next to you, by the well.'

'I didn't see any child. There are no children here.'

'But I've seen children. Playing football.'

'Oh! Some children come from town to visit their grandmothers during the weekends. Yes, sorry.'

'So?'

'So what?'

'The child, she was right there!'

'I'm sorry; I haven't seen her.'

She went back to her house and looked out from the window. On the other side, the world was a hell of frozen architecture, with a tall, thin girl next to the well, stubbornly looking at her. She didn't go out again to confront her. She knew the girl would become a tree in the distance, broken in two. Or some pole or other. Or a crimson shirt caught up in a makeshift fence.

5.

She had a dream. She was picking mushrooms in an unknown forest. They were red and tempting through the mist and the foliage; she knew they were dangerous, poisonous, that she should not take them. But she couldn't resist their brightness.

He would only have what he deserved, what was his due. She thought: I'll feed him the mushrooms. He would never know, won't feel a thing.

What a fierce thing was she, a jilted woman.

An animal came out of the thick fog, but she could not see whether it was sheep or wolf.

6.

The metallic noise woke her up. Through the back window she saw that someone had knocked over the rubbish bins. Some of the old ladies were probably taking more wood for their stoves. Why didn't they simply ask her for some? she thought crossly.

She had fallen asleep with the television on with the sound off. It was completely unnecessary; the colours of the programme shouted around the room, clamouring for attention.

The pinks and reds and yellows gave way to the sombre colours of the news report. A woman with a jacket was showing:

a little girl's picture, a child really, nine or ten years old, last seen in a little red hood

an artist's rendition of the man suspected to have taken her

a long number requesting information, long digits red as blood, cutting the screen in two

Stupidly, the first thing that came to mind was that the television stations still existed. Until then she had thought that someone was left alone there, feeding videos of old programmes into a never-ending loop.

The second thought was for reality, collapsing.

She came back to herself, still in shock, looked for the remote, found it, put the volume back up.

Calm down, she thought, calm down. It cannot be. But inside her head there was a little train in a little station in the middle of nowhere, about to crash into bits.

She heard him then, entering through the back door. She heard him pour himself a glass of the brownish water. Water they ought to be thankful for having, she knew, though it tasted of decay and death. Of course it did. What else could it taste of?

She switched off the set and walked out.

She didn't know how long she had been walking. Ahead of her, the tall pines of the Andalusian forest seemed to melt into one another. At the end of her vision, the still landscape lost its colours in a blur of light and whiteness.

She felt the need to get off the path, to get lost. It wouldn't be so bad after all.

She understood that the snow is somehow alive, and would drag her away, whether she wanted it or not.

Did the cure work, the cure for love-sickness? Is he dead now, far away in the distant city? A factory accident waiting to happen, run over by a military truck?

And then she knew it: it was she who was about to disappear.

She sat on the wet ground, concentrating on a certain point, a black tree standing against the background. She felt sleepy. And she thought that her dead body would not smell at all, deciding at once that was much better than rotting inside a well.

7.

They looked at each other in silence. The wolf had really small eyes, she thought, and a bluish hue to its skin. It continued playing with the scraps it had taken from her rubbish. Behind his silhouette, elegant, utter perfection, the sunset was like a huge serving plate of orange china, so beautiful that she burst into tears.

What am I doing here? she thought.

The wolf turned round and left, without turning to look at her once, back into the depths of the sierra.

Black Isle

0001

THE OSPREYS' DEATHS—BY THE DOZENS—ARE inexplicable, as is the bluish taint on their beaks, heads and chests. It simply should not be there. I should know, for I designed the birds.

Every morning, day breaks over the mudflats, covered in osprey corpses and unexpected bluish reflections, as if a hundred will-o-the-wisps of the wrong colour were advancing over the watery surface. The smooth flat mirror of the mudflats shines indigo: fluorescent, freakish, *wrong*. From their beaks, and from sores on their chests and bellies, there pours a tainted viscous liquid that resembles watery gelatine, odourless and sticky to the touch.

This is, of course, not what our star product for the Scottish ecosystem should do. Our fabricated birds, to start with, should not die this soon, a mere fifteen years after their release into nature. They are engineered: to sustain longer life, eternal in some cases, to maintain fish and insect numbers—a delicate dance of environmental equilibrium.

'Dr Hay, your presence is required, code A-001.'

A summons from God himself. I cannot recall being asked to Philip's office since our last disagreement, and that was months ago. But I do what I'm told. Things are changing, and I am now treated by everyone as a newcomer, an embarrassing uncle. No one seems to remember that at the beginning it was me, and Philip, and Barbara, fighting against the elements. Fighting against those who believed our work unethical. I risked as much as he did, more in fact. Barbara risked it all.

'Thank you, Dolores.'

I close the intercom, walk towards the cabinet, and slide open its glass doors with a light wave of my hand. I find the bottle of vodka behind a row of gold-tooled volumes, and take it gently to my lips with a furtive movement: the light is flashing red by a corner of the ceiling, little rubies of a warning. I'm being observed.

0002

The green rocks and hills of the Highlands reflect the yellow glow of the bio-engineered grass, and the landscape shines on the other side of the glass and white-aluminium dome. The colossal hall, built to the proportions of our greatest achievement to date, the de-extinct monolithic squid, is a vast oblong chamber of pure whiteness into which the landscape pours its new colours. On sunnier days the yellow and orange reflections are almost unbearable, and the glass octahedrons taint themselves a shade or two darker to keep us sheltered. This part of Scotland can be particularly hot during the winter months.

The dome resembles a hive made of the glass panels supported by white aluminium, a triumph of de-modernized architecture imitating late twenty-first century design. The vast column of the aquarium occupies its centre, placed there to greet the visitors with our impressive bio-engineered reproductions: sharks, whales, dolphins, coral, moonfish. The squid moves gracefully among its fellow inmates as I walk round the watery cylinder. It takes me seventeen minutes to complete the circle. I notice new species locked in there. Apparently we have starfish now. Only the natural-correct colours, in accordance with the Scottish Law on Bio-Ethics and the International Consensus on De-Extinction. We pride ourselves on reproducing environments; no one is interested here in the new fashions for violet sheep or pink cows. We leave these frivolities as the pets of rich Russians.

Philip's office has its own private elevator, as well as another entry-escape route: a helipad on its balcony. I press the only button in the white capsule. The answer comes back in flashing red; it has been a while since I have been granted direct access to him.

Two members of the security staff push the doors open to find me there.

'Sorry, sir,' one of them says, their attitude relaxing a bit. They have obviously been briefed. They put down their white machine-guns, one of them presses the button again, and the system reacts, positively this time, to his DNA.

The doors close and the elevator moves upwards.

0003

Philip is standing behind his desk when I enter. His office is immaculately white, as is everything else in XenoLab.

The genetically-engineered Siberian tiger, re-imagined by Neo-Bio to be as tame and lazy as a gigantic housecat, is stretching in the middle of the chamber, causing echoes as he plays with a worn-out red plastic sphere. I cross the vast space, cavernous with the sounds of the beast, and those of my own shoes over the white marble.

'Andrew, dear friend,' Philip's voice resonates. His hair and his trimmed beard are also white now, I notice, in communion with our corporate surroundings.

'Philip. You wanted to see me.' I hope I don't sound like an obedient child.

He looks down, turns awkwardly and advances towards the glass wall on the south side of the chamber. He looks diminutive with his hands behind

60

his back, looking through the glass in the direction of the distant aviary, an external structure of gigantic proportions, shaped like a huge pine cone.

'How have you been?'

I would like to imagine that there is some genuine interest in his tone of voice. But I know my ex-business partner well enough not to hold false illusions. Nonetheless, his question brings Barbara's face back to my mind. It was probably designed to do exactly that, throw salt into the old wound, and I hate him for it.

'Marvellous.' There's no point hiding the lie. 'What's up, Philip?'

He cannot see the birds from where he stands. It is obvious he's looking in the direction of the cone to avoid turning to face me.

'The ospreys were one of our first, were they not?' he says laconically. I notice he still speaks the same way, ending sentences with a negative answer. Manipulation 101.

'That is correct.'

'I am sorry to say this requires swift action. We cannot allow the reputation of our company to be affected.'

Our company.

'What do you propose to do?'

'Go there, back to Black Isle, and take a small team of your choosing. Find out what is wrong with the birds.'

'Why me?'

'I need someone I can trust.' I believe him, God knows why. Perhaps because I want to believe him, even after everything that has happened.

'Why are a bunch of birds so important, Philip? What aren't you telling me?'

He turns and smiles briefly, more with his squinting eyes than with his mouth.

'Nothing, old friend, nothing.' Now he is the one who doesn't bother to hide the lie. 'But they were some of our first, were they not?' he repeats.

His meaning dawns on me at last. I never had his powers of memory, and it's been fifteen years. Fifteen years in which I have had reason enough to forget.

I reply that I'll do all in my power, turning in the direction of the elevator. Before leaving I specify that I will go on my own. He does not refuse me this small request, the only victory I contemplate gaining anytime soon. I savour it in silence.

'Andrew,' he calls as the elevator doors are closing. I push them open, and wait for him to speak. 'Mendez has already been there.' This surprises me. I thought I had kept myself informed of the company's recent goings-on. It had obviously been a secret outing. 'He went and returned with no conclusive results. You should seek him out, talk to him.'

'Of course, I will do so first thing.' I let the doors go.

'Andrew!' I put my foot just in time once more between the doors before they close.

'Yes, Philip?' My tone is ironic, disdainful. Each one of us is back in his proper place, and mine is obviously that of the delivery boy.

He looks in my direction again, advancing towards the elevator. I did not expect this; I tense unexpectedly. Even at a distance he looks haggard, strangely old. I wonder if my ex-friend has stopped following his rejuvenating bio-treatments. 'Mendez is in Hospital Zero Zero Sixteen. Committed. Mental ward.' The matter-of-fact manner with which he delivers this piece of significant information freezes me out. I leave at last.

The elevator takes me back down into the hall. This time I fancy that I see a bluish foam coming out of the whale's mouth as she exhales. There is nothing there. It is only a reflection of a rare passing cloud over the cylindrical structure, staining the glass with its dark shadow.

0004

I am alone in bed. Dolores has just left me and gone back to her own compound. I get up, go to the bathroom and splash my face with cold water.

I open my computer and connect myself to the company hive. 'Black Isle,' I say to the screen that waits flat like the surface of calm stagnant water. The requested information starts popping up fast over the screen, reports and charts and scientific articles, and I am startled by the number of species that we have introduced into that particular environment.

Not only birds, but fish and mammals as well. Insects, some species genetically engineered to help decimate the rapidly multiplying ones. Genetically modified grass, the kind that won't miss the disappearing clouds. Flowers. I wonder how much of the landscape is fake in the place, how much of it remains original, if any.

Close to us, Black Isle was one of our first proving-grounds. A small peninsula twenty minutes to the west of Inverness, it is placed right in front of the vast watery expanse of the Bauly Firth in the North Sea. On the opposite shore, the hills and the glens of The Aird are visible in the distance, with its farmland and its pretty copses, a soft mist dancing over the small summits.

The Bauly Firth is an unusual spot. The place is subjected to dramatic changes in its ecosystem every few hours following the tides. For half a day, twice a day, the water recedes, and an expanse of mudflats extends itself further into the distance, crossing the whole bay and reaching the Aird, a strange black mirror filled with the inevitable quicksands, a deceptive landscape that looks barren but that is full of life. I notice this landscape of an entire bay without water has been referred to in the company reports somehow unflatteringly as "a long view of a lot of mud."

The mud houses a particular type of animal life. Afterwards, in a mere few hours, the water reconquers it all with its undulating dark glimmer. It is then when

64

the birds reappear, together with certain types of fish, seals, dolphins, crossing the bay in direction to Inverness. Enormous hen harriers and cormorants, diving gracefully into the water to hunt their prey, small martens running around, birds coming and going, ever-changing, as subtly as the rhythms of the water. The place is utterly fascinating for a biologist. The bay becomes a completely different biological environment in each of its distinctive phases.

Black Isle is also one of many self-contained late twenty-first century environments, protected by its own glass and aluminium dome. The company will organise the necessary paperwork to grant me access.

The ospreys were not simply one of our first; they were our first one hundred per cent success story. After the ospreys, everything else came swiftly, easily, and Neo-Bio took a massive leap forward. Everything changed. We weren't ready, when the birds first disappeared, for our ecosystem's metamorphosis: but we could see the danger it posed to our species. Hundreds of birds suffered a sudden decline in numbers, vanishing at the same time as their main food, small insects, multiplied in dangerous proportions. The swarms destroyed lives, destroyed property. The latter was determinant in making the powers that be act.

Maintaining the insect eaters constant became XenoLab's first mission. After the success with the ospreys, that was our next job, to re-imagine the insects-eaters with a supra-hunger. Success after success, our reputation grew without equal. We were like God himself, reestablishing the balance in His creation.

I remember the day we freed the ospreys. They all had a white tag embedded in their legs, shiny, easy to spot with binoculars.

0005

I glide over the avenues and the open squares, marvelling as always at the daring of some of our competitors. I ascertain, even from manoeuvring-height, that the new fashion for taking polar bears as pets has reached our city, as has the one that prizes giant lizards, tigers, and other unusual animals for human company. My opinion about this hasn't changed: it does not matter how tame these beasts have been re-imagined by Neo-Bio, it is obvious that this new fashion for modifying the instincts of species not suited for human company has to pose some kind of danger.

At least the Scottish Republic's law spares us from the blue bears, the orange lizards. I will not be able to stand seeing them around when they are legally available, which will surely happen eventually.

I negotiate the narrow entry into the parking dock at the block where the hospital is located. I do not know this area of the city well, but my vehicle has brought me in with the autopilot. It is a new model provided by the company, a convertible which will also run over ground once I am granted access to the domed zone of Black Isle.

I show my credentials and am ushered quickly to the exact place by a young assistant doctor. I am impressed by the effectiveness and power that a card from XenoLab still commands.

The hospital is as white as every other building in the city—Scotland still misses, all these decades later, its snowy winter landscapes—but I am led through one white corridor after another until we reach a back area outside of the main wards, and here the paint is peeling, the plumbing is exposed over the walls and the lights flick, covering each turn in increasing darkness.

We stop in front of a metal door with a hatch for food. The door is unlocked. I am pushed in, the door locked again quickly after me.

The place is hardly illuminated by an orange bulb. Mendez is a formless bundle in one corner.

'Mendez?' There's no answer. 'Mendez?'

He turns and finally sees me. He tries to focus his eyes on me, tries to recognise me.

'I am waiting for him.'

'Who?'

'My master.'

'Do you mean Philip?'

He looks up, and crawls closer. He has aged beyond recognition. His rejuvenation program had stopped him at age twenty-four. He looks nearly forty now, or perhaps fifty. It is difficult to know.

'God,' he says simply. Just before I ask again if he is talking about Philip, he utters a few words that I don't quite catch, and takes something into his mouth.

He is eating flies. I don't even know where from. There are no flies—not officially at least—under the city's dome.

'What have you said?' I ask.

'Pan. I am waiting for him.'

I do not have a clue what he is talking about, but understand I will get no useful information. His mind seems to be gone completely.

As I'm turning round, I hear the loud thump, wettish and sudden, of meat hitting the wall. It is followed by a distant whining, some lonely animal conjured up into this narrow chamber to devour us. I do not want to turn back, but I do. The blood has already formed a miniature lake, darker than redder, and Mendez is convulsing on the floor. There is no animal there, unless he is the animal. But I know that animals do not harm themselves. I am pushed to one side unceremoniously as the attendants get in. I do not desire to see the outcome to my visit, and escape quickly through the open door. I can't feel pity, not now; I'm sorry for Mendez, but I've seen enough to pity him.

0006

I stay with Peter and Anita, the allocated occupants of Pier Cottage, exactly like I did fifteen years ago.

68

The house enjoys a privileged situation, a mere five minutes walk from the Gothic ruins of Red Castle, a small turreted structure abandoned to rot at the end of the twentieth century when its owner decided he could not pay more taxes on the property and removed the roof to stop is mounting debt to the government.

On the right side of the cottage there is a path that leads into the old quarry, with its oddly flat and reddish walls cut into the hill. The house and the Castle are both built out of this local stone, as it is the abandoned Victorian pier that gives its name to the cottage, put there in order to transport the stone from the quarry into Inverness over the bay. The pier's abandonment means it is no more than an overgrown greenish and rocky structure that advances into the water, hard to walk over, and which gets dangerously covered by the regular tides.

Apart from the striking landscape, and the Gothic ruin of Red Castle, Black Isle is particularly rich in Megalithic chambered cairns. It was inhabited in 3000 BC by prehistoric men, and New Stone Age folk constructed these tomb-buildings. There seems to be two main types on the isle, the Orkney and the Clava, one rectangular and one a stone ring, with a circular burial chamber underground. I promise myself to visit some before my field trip is over, something I did not manage to do during the release-trip all those years ago.

Everything is pretty much unchanged over the past fifteen years. Anita's cat startles me as much as it did back then, its red eyes marking him out as one of the first, discarded models of genetic manufacture of the old days, re-imagined not to attack the birds but unsuccessful in every other aspect. Everything is pretty much the same, including Anita. Her smile still awakens something in me. The way she looks at me makes me think that she hasn't entirely forgotten our brief affair.

The place is quite magical, utterly unspoiled. That is, unspoiled but at present subtly different from what it was, due to the interaction of companies such as ours with the landscape, *precisely* so as to keep it unspoiled. It is strangely unreal, this truthful version of a late twenty-first century Scottish ecosystem. The irony does not escape me. It has been my major point of conflict with Philip in recent times.

The green expanses reflect the yellow glow of the genetically engineered grass. Once the motorway crosses the bridge over the water, you find yourself negotiating narrow winding country roads framed by little stone walls, trees and thickets. Some of the moss over the fake walls is also fabricated. I can see it plainly even from the moving vehicle.

From the window of the kitchen one can observe even without binoculars the birds that come to the feeders, mostly chaffinch, greenfinch, blue tits, bullfinch and a rare young woodpecker. Several of these birds are of our own manufacture, as an inspection with the binoculars reveals the white tags in their legs, shining with their unusual plastic glimmer. Not the woodpecker, however. He seems the genuine article.

0008

We walk over to the pier. To reach its end a short walk is necessary, no more than three hundred metres, but I am soon reminded how hard is to advance over the abandoned structure. The overgrown reeds and the muddy grass have covered it all. The seaweed climbs onto it from its deceptive little shores. But the worst is that the remaining rocks of the man-built pier are now out of place and out of shape, as if a giant had scattered the original square stones from the sky without looking to see where they would fall. Time and abandonment have covered them in the green of the reeds and the grass, so much so that it is impossible to find steady ground, or even to avoid holes and uneven spots where it would be easy to twist one's ankle.

We need nearly half an hour to get to its rounded end.

Halfway onto the pier, the grass is spotted here and there with the corpses of crabs of different sizes. They are all the same kind of local specimen, and they are all tainted with the irregular bluish-green. I collect several of them, and some of the bluish-tainted grass around their emptied bodies. The cottage is provided with a small working lab, well enough equipped to carry out small tasks. Anita is carrying plastic sample bags. Peter is taking digital photographs for my initial report, for which these notes are intended. They both have been most helpful.

I see a figure over the mud, and I put my binoculars to my eyes: a man is dragging a net-fishing bag full of what I can make out as the huge cadavers of birds, bleeding their cobalt liquid into the darkened mirror of the mud as he walks.

'Who is that?' I ask.

'Oh no. Good gracious!'

Peter advances to the uneven border of the pier and starts shouting at the man.

'McKenzie! You're going to drown, you stupid son of a bitch!'

I am startled by his reaction. I remember Peter as an educated, mild-mannered, retired science teacher. He turns in my direction and explains.

'Tomorrow morning those birds will be laid at our door.'

'What?'

I am not offered an explanation as to how the man McKenzie, who is braving the quicksand in such reckless fashion, knows of Peter and Anita's connection to XenoLab, or why he directs the birds' death towards the inhabitants of Pier Cottage. Or how much he knows about our de-extinction work in the area. But that he is angry at us is clear.

Later in the day we observe the tide covering the mud, rapidly filling the Bay, splashing around the pier. The remains of the structure get completely covered except for its round tip. I make a mental note to find out the tide times as soon as possible; it is more than likely that venturing onto the pier again will be needed, and I do not desire to get stranded there with the vicious winds and the vicious seagulls.

I see the man McKenzie is walking along the shore, dragging behind him his trophy of dead fabricated birds.

0009

I am thinking of how quiet this new nature has turned out to be. There are hardly any bird sounds, an unexpected silence. I know by memory the osprey's call, as described in my field guide: *A short, cheeping whistle, sometimes slightly declining.* I guess I can remember it; I certainly can imagine a sound described like that. But I haven't heard it once here, and it has been a while since I've heard it anywhere else.

What I have seen is their clear white bellies, the black wing patches, when the birds glide overhead. I have seen them, alive and flying; and I have also by now collected their cadavers and dissected them by the dozens. The man McKenzie has not graced us so far with his grim reaping, despite Peter's assurances that he would.

Evening approaches, and my hosts must be preparing dinner. I am out for an evening walk after one of the dissecting sessions, trying to regain my appetite with some much-needed fresh air. Almost by impulse I turn at the last moment in a two-way path and venture into Red Castle's abandoned grounds. I reach the structure, inspect the plaque on the wall, inscribed with the date 1641, and look over the Bauly Firth, the bay in front of me in its formidable vastness. I admire the Castle's defensive position. I decide to push into the extensive woods and come out on the other side of my hosts' home. I trust my instinct not to get lost, and cross eventually into the area of the old farmlands, now covered in decorative crops.

Barbara would have liked this contrasting landscape. I bury the thought as deep as possible.

Something is shinning blue on the Castle's grounds. It's a hare, or a rat. It is difficult to ascertain, as all there remains is a furry wet pulp of flesh, and something that looks like a strange bluish-green gelatine.

I pack the remains of the animal into a sample bag and carry it back home with me.

OOIO

I am in bed when I hear a dry bump against the main door. I look out of my window but see nothing. The next morning Anita shows me a robin, dead from the collision with the door of Pier Cottage. Inside his breast a bluish heart is shining. The right leg displays its whitish plastic tag.

My notes from the previous trip to Black Isle are little more than useless. Apart from the observations of the releasing day proper, they contain nothing helpful. The acquired wisdom of observations relating to the weather. Indications for sowing the seed, for when to begin harvesting. Customs outmoded now, since we have completely eradicated hunger with our genetically engineered crops, destroyed death and illness with the widely available rejuvenating processes.

I remember those nights in which Anita explained these wonders to me: that tomorrow's weather starts to be foretold the previous evening, that if swallows fly high in their search for insects there will be good weather. If the cattle bunch together in a corner of the field, rain may be expected.

There is only nice weather now; it was one the first things man learned to interact with. Our satellites, strategically placed around the globe, provide a never-ending provision of cloudless skies, mild temperatures, constant and bright sunshine.

If the lights of the Aurora Borealis, or *Merry Dancers*, sweep across the sky, and Scottish countryfolk can see them from their homes, disturbed weather is on the way. I do not know very well what the Aurora Borealis is. Must find records on the company hive; I remember clearly making the same promise to Anita fifteen years ago, while I noted down all these. I obviously wasn't interested enough, and only took notes on these useless bits of local information as a means to flirt with her.

Fifteen years ago, Barbara waited for me back home. There had not yet been any renal failure, no transplant from the genetically-engineered pigs, performed strictly against her religious wishes, and no final rejection of the animal's harvested organ by her body. Fifteen years ago we had not managed to crack that side of our business, I'm afraid, and Barbara was little more than an experiment for Philip, a stoat, small but vicious, a little guinea pig.

Red rowan berries protect against witches. Some flowers (broom, hawthorn, foxglove) should never be taken into the houses. Robins have a drop of God's blood in its veins. It is unlucky to hurt one of them for that reason.

Barbara would have said that God himself was angry with us, producing the blue viscous liquid. Was Jesus's blood meant to be bluish? Or was that what was said about kings and queens in the tales of the old days? I wish I had kept the meaning of these things buried in some field notebook. I wish I had my own archive, my own private hive, my personal stack of useless knowledge from past days.

When I see him is too late to hide. The stone circle, in the middle of a round, dark meadow, half covered by the treetops falling on it from its side, offers no other hiding place than the actual cairn that I have come to visit, which turns out to be a mound with a little excavation entrance. I glance over it; it seems blocked, or rather leading nowhere. It is too late anyhow to escape. Are the Neolithic tombs also a decoration, perhaps? No time to muse about it.

'Morning,' I say.

'Morning,' he answers. He stops in front of me, and says nothing else. He has his hands in his pockets.

Attack is as good a defence as any and, since I've got the notion that he considers me the enemy, I waste no time.

'I guess you know who I am, and what I am doing here.'

He smiles crookedly but says nothing, taken aback by my forwardness no doubt.

'Oh yes, I know who you are,' he says at last.

'And how can I help you?'

'Oh, no, you cannot help me... You cannot help us.'

This is leading nowhere. I start again:

'Look, man... McKenzie, isn't it?'

'I just want to show you something.'

I am not surprised by his offer. I had expected something similar to these: proofs of the company's mismanagement of the environment, threats of dismal intensity, perhaps just expecting some kind of compensation, maybe in the form of rejuvenating credit.

'Very well,' I say at last. 'I'll come.'

We head deep into the woods, leaving the quarry behind. Very soon there is no sight of the sea, although it can clearly be heard from practically everywhere in Black Isle due to the lack of animal noise I have already noted. The sound of the water makes me feel strangely at ease.

His cabin is quite well kept, a fresh lick of whitewash on the walls, recently fixed wooden fences.

He takes me towards the back, into a small working hut. I wonder who this man is, why he is allowed inside the dome, what role he performs, if any, on Black Isle. I gather that he has what are called 'historical rights'—that is to say, his family has always belonged to the area and therefore he can stay. A controversial idea. But I cannot imagine any other way in which he would be allowed to be here, in the middle of our delicately engineered dance.

He opens the door and then I see it.

There is absolutely no smell, but the animals, of all sizes and shapes, are the bluish mash I have half expected. Shockingly, not only birds. A bucket is filled with what looks like different kinds of insects and rodents. The birds are hanging upside down. At the back of the hut there is a dead blue-sheep lying on a worktable. I have no idea such large species have also been affected. I turn round in disbelief.

'Where did you find her?' I asked.

'She was mine, my sheep.' That is all the information he offers.

When I leave I am asking myself two questions. What have we done here, and what should we do next?

OO13

I finish and send my report. The experiments I have conducted with Anita's help have formulated no final theory, although I am still waiting on the samples I have sent Philip's way. But I really see no way to stop this extravagant virus, which is not a virus, but which seems nonetheless to be spreading all over the area at a level I could not have anticipated. The animals themselves seem to be carrying this possibility of de-continuation. I offer no possible solution. There is none until we look in more detail into the issue. I recommend the creation of a research team back in XenoLab to start working with immediate effect. Secretly, of course. I understand the sensitivity of the issue. My final prediction is to expect more cases outside of this particular dome, quite soon.

The cat is staring at me with his 'evil' fake red eyes. He comes and rubs himself against my leg and I shudder. I go to sleep and my mind is uneasy, heavy images of what I have been shown hanging on me. I dream of Barbara, of the days prior to her operation.

I was privately offered another option before that fatal day: one experimental dose of proto-phomaldeion to keep her in animated suspension, living eternally, until the xeno was not experimental anymore and we had better results with the harvesting of organs from animals. I never got to see the huge capsule where the substance would be provided, but in my dream a blue syrup is injected into her small arm, and Barbara cries blue tears as the liquid fills her up.

Philip is also crying blue tears while his face, no longer treated with the rejuvenation process, collapses into old age all of a sudden, in front of my very eyes, while he communicates to me her passing.

I wake up covered in cold sweat, and wet with tears, thinking about xeno-suspension, xeno-cloning and other rapidly progressing issues I simply cannot cope with, but which nonetheless are under way, even in the minutes of the Scottish parliament's Bio-Regulation Commission's latest meetings. I lie in bed thinking that, perhaps, Philip has been right to cast me away from the front line of things. I am an old-fashioned man, typing these notes with my fingers on my computer instead of talking into it, collecting field notebooks written with ink, or rather a succedaneum of ink manufacture by myself, since it is impossible to buy it. A man unable, as it were, to accept the realities that surround me. Perhaps I should commission a shiny red goat as a pet and snap out of it once and for all.

Philip has read my report and demands to talk with me through HiveCam. I do not have my profile active anymore, although that goes strictly against company regulations. I then receive a strange message through an encoded email provider, contracted during the early days of the company, and which we used to communicate delicate matters. We have not used it to talk in years. I am confused when I see the red flag on my screen, until I suddenly remember what it means.

I command the computer to open the message. I am even more confused after reading it: 'Code Z-666'. Get out. Leave. Abort. I've always prided myself on knowing the company's code-protocols by heart. I helped write them, after all.

I trust I'll find the cabin of the man McKenzie. I trust that I will not get lost. I reach without problem the stone circle with its Neolithic tomb, and from there I try to reorient myself. I do reach the cabin, and the hut, eventually. I hardly notice the twilight, which is nothing more than a pale-grey sky miles higher, beyond the distant dome.

'You're back.'

It's a statement, and affirmation. I walk in the direction of the strange man.

'What do you want?'

'Talk, just to talk.'

I am not sure what kind of help I expect to get from him, but if nothing else I want his assistance to conduct a larger survey of Black Isle. I'm also carrying the digital camera, and want to ask permission to photograph the animals in his hut. For now, I let myself be led into the cabin, where the man flicks on the electric kettle.

He rinses a few herbs and puts them inside a teapot. He then pours the water.

'Do you take sugar?'

I say no. He puts some in my cup anyway. The infusion is still acidic in my tongue.

'Do you want any of this?' he says holding a small bottle of whisky. I say no, wishing it was vodka instead.

'What do you think is happening here?' I ask.

He shrugs for an answer, but says:

'Nature will reconquer, will she not?'

I am startled for a second. Something unexpected has happened: the way he has spoken has reminded me of Philip.

'She will battle back,' he continues, in his dark Scottish drawl.

I look into his eyes, and then I see it. Philip's eyes, his nose. In a body twenty years his senior. What the hell is going on here?

I get up and go towards an old-fashioned static-photograph on the wall, where two children are showing the animals they've hunted to the camera, each of them holding a huge bird by the legs. The Bauly Firth's mudflats shine behind them.

I turn to say something more, but I feel unexpectedly dizzy. My vision blurs, and I try to find something to grab.

The herbs. I am a biologist. I suddenly recognise the herbs he has made me drink. I think I've seen a hedge of it outside, with its horny stems and foxglove-like flowers. *Datura stramonium.*

Thorn apple, devil's apple, devil's trumpet, feuille du diable, herb du diable, green thorn apple.

I fall to the floor at last. I look up, and a blurry image walks in my direction. McKenzie. Or rather a re-imagined version of the man McKenzie, completed with hooves and horns and the face of a sheep.

I close my eyes to the hallucination, and doze happily into oblivion.

Z-666

Thorn apple, devil's apple, devil's trumpet, feuille du diable, herb du diable, green thorn apple. Datura stramonium. Get out. Leave. Abort. She is running in my direction. Behind her, the red ruin of the Castle is shedding blue tears. I'm crying, but my hands get cover in the same indigo slime when I touch my face. She is running, but is not her; or rather, it is an older version of my wife, as if she had declined our rejuvenating credit. Barbara gets to where I am and slaps my face with the full force of her rage. She is shouting now. Zero Zero Sixteen. Zero Zero Sixteen. Wake up. Wake up!

I wake up cold, uncomfortable, wet. It takes me a few seconds to understand where I am, lying at the very end of the pier. The tide is coming in, in full spate. I notice that there is water all around me. Only the rounded end where I have been dropped is not covered by it. There is no escape now until the tide goes down.

I see them then: hundreds and thousands of dead fish, floating over the grey-bluish surface. Then the birds start falling from the sky.

Behind me, a huge roar announces that the trees in the Castle's grounds are collapsing as well.

Everything is dying, at the exact same moment. As if someone had orchestrated it all, or pushed the required button from a safe and distant location.

I notice the sea is exploding: here, where it has always been an unmoving mirror of greyness.

From the sea, an enormous whale is coming in my direction. Where from? How did she get into the domed space? Only it doesn't look like a whale, exactly. It looks like a shapeless monster, bleeding its blue foam as it advances into the pier.

I try to remember a prayer, but I can't.

I close my eyes and think of Barbara, her image slapping my face, through a rare moment of clarity. Not in the domed Black Isle, not in my compound.

Am I still here? Or am I with Mendez?

Zero Zero Sixteen.

The reality is too harsh to contemplate. I close my eyes once more, and I'm back there, alone in the pier. The whale opens her mouth, and prepares to swallow me up.

STONES

THE FIRST TIME RAVEN SAW THE BOY WITH GLASSES AND strawberry-blond hair, she had gone to the meadow with her backpack full of books, two oranges and her Walkman. She was lying with her shoes off against the rounded granite of one of the smallest rocks, right in front of the copse. She loved sitting on the soft bed of liverwort and moss punctuated by heather. It was her favourite spot inside the stone circle. The stone where she lay inclined towards the west, catching whatever sun was left at that hour.

When she saw him emerging from the copse in her direction her heartbeat quickened. He crossed the meadow, deliberately not looking at her. He was carrying a book. She blushed and then she felt it; it was an odd sensation, warm and unexpected, which will never fail to appear in successive days, every time their paths crossed in the main street, or when they met at the newsagent on the corner of Regency with St. Albans' Road. On those occasions their eyes would lock for one second, and she would be swamped again by that warm, inexplicable feeling of wanting to stay forever locked into that look.

The stones covered the meadow unevenly. Depending on where you stood, their circular formation revealed itself, and it was possible to get a better sense of them. Some stones were longer or bigger than others, and they were all made of different rocks from different quarries from all over the county. The central stone was the only one made of quartz. It knelt at an impossible angle, long and pointed. It looked as if it were resting on thin air. They resembled three maidens dancing around the central quartz rock.

They seemed to have been there from the beginning of time itself, silently absorbing their force from everything around them. They had been there even before there had been a town, even before the county had been called a county, since that stretch of land was nothing more than a round mound of earth with the remains of a prehistoric settlement, round houses and round barns, with a magnetic spot at its centre. They were a man-made monument in praise of the town's riches: quartz, coal, ether. Hers was a mining town, serving the hungry needs of civilization.

The fact that the stones celebrated those treasures made her feel uneasy. She could feel the indefinite energy with which the stones filled the valley, extending itself over the brown pastures and remaining fields. She had come to regard the circle as an impure, odd thing. Raven secretly liked this idea. She kept coming back to the stones, hoping to see the strawberry-blond boy with glasses, hoping for her heartbeat to quicken, hoping to be overcome by the rush, the warm feeling. And perhaps, she thought, to have *the thing* that had already happened to every single girl in her class happening to her at last. The fear that it would *never* happen was simply too much to contemplate.

In the meadow one could almost imagine something close to silence taking place. Over the hilltops the distant humming of the North, South, East and West colossal Pit Heads, buzzing and clamping noises hour after hour, echoed through the valley. The men and the women in the town forced out of the rock the precious means of energy, tearing them apart from Earth itself, and she somehow knew that it could not be at no cost. This she knew: there was hardly anything unnatural in her world, no power to will the strawberry-blond boy to reappear, no matter how hard she tried it. The stones represented, encapsulated, whatever ancient power remained. But it was a dark power, uncertain. If she was to believe her family lore, it had been different even for her mother, a mere generation back. She felt the pang of absence acutely, the fact that her mother was there no more to guide her, to explain things to her.

Perhaps this was what getting older meant, realising that you cannot fix everything.

The meadow was one of the few unspoiled areas remaining. Mining had silently conquered it all, covering the ground and the sky in an indistinct greyness. The town sat deep in a valley kept in perpetual shade by the slope and the interrupted, uneven hills, all of them crowned by the monstrous Pit Heads, opening their black iron mouths to swallow the young people up.

The stones and the meadow were also one of the few blind spots for the Eye, the town's camera obscura, designed to find those few who defied progress. She knew the circles it described in its rotatory march by heart in its endless overseeing of life in the city. She had been born in the family who manipulated it, and would grow up to invigilate the streets herself.

Not in the meadow. There she was safe to do as she wanted.

The sun was setting. In a moment the moon would cover the stones with its pale glow, and the formation would resemble more closely the enchanted castle she had imagined it to be when she was a child. It was almost time to go home, to the familiarity of the broken chair in the kitchen, the dim light in the downstairs bathroom, the bedroom window that didn't close properly, the town's Eye in the fake tower. Falling asleep to the distant lullaby of the television set. The theme tune of the news, the sirens from police cars, the anger of the demonstrators, the metallic nasal voice of the Iron Lady, enraged, shouting about those ungrateful miners who might indeed bring Great Britain to its final destruction. The muffled ranting always made her feel safe, less alone up in her bedroom.

She had left the meadow and was walking downhill when she felt it in the air, even before she saw it: the colossal Southern Pit Head, the one extracting ether, enveloped in flames as huge as the structure, turning the countryside as hot as the pit of hell, and the bumblebee helicopters rushing to extinguish them through the flashing red beams of light.

———

'Hi, kid!'

She had never seen this girl before, but she had come out of her house.

'Hi.'

She was wearing a t-shirt with 'The Sex-Pistons' printed on it, and her hair was a succession of alternate green and blue spikes, resting over a mostly shaved head. Raven wondered if the girl would have to bend down to get through the doorway. It turned out that she did.

'I'm Port, your second cousin twice-removed. I've come to help with the Eye,' said the girl.

'What kind of name is *that*?' She wasn't just being rude; she knew that there was no way she could get along with this girl. She wondered idly if her stupid uncle thought she needed was a babysitter.

'It's short for Portia.'

Raven's eyes lit up. Portia was her favourite name out of all the possible Shakespearean favourite names that she had. Portia was clever and funny and wise. Portia saved the fucking day, that's what Portia did.

'Your name is *Portia*?'

'Yep. My parents are bookish types, I'm afraid... You can call me Port. Everyone calls me Port. It's loads easier. What do you have for breakfast, normally?'

This took Raven aback. The succession of Eye assistants had never asked what she wanted for breakfast, or even suggested to have it with her.

'Erm... Toast with Marmite? Tea?'

Portia's face contracted as a wave of disgust blew over her heavily made-up face. She ducked her tongue out for extra emphasis.

'Marmite? Are you fucking kidding me?'

Raven could not help a little smile.

'Man! Who the fuck invented that shit? It's *salty mud*! It's the most disgusting thing in the whole fucking universe!'

Raven cracked up with laughter. She made herself stop, uneasy. She knew what the presence of Portia meant: more hours of searching, looking for the saboteurs.

The pattern was readily established. Port would arrive at eight thirty on her bike, and they would have breakfast together. Then Raven read or did her vacation homework while Port climbed up to the tower and worked the lens of the camera obscura, covering the whole town in a few minutes, and start again. Despite her looks, she didn't seem to have a problem telling on people, and the report vacuum tubes kept their healthy activity. Now and then she would smoke a cigarette in the back garden, an unkempt patch of dirty grass with a few empty flowerbeds and a laurel hedge that badly needed pruning. By the time she offered a cigarette to Raven, one of the flowerbeds was covered with a thin layer of butts.

'Your uncle said that you tried to escape a couple of times when you were little.'

Raven didn't reply. She concentrated with all her might on not choking on the cigarette.

'Why did you do that? You could have got lost.'

'That was the aim,' she answered with a smirk.

Portia took a long drag, pressed the cigarette against the wall of the house and threw the butt in the flowerbed with the others.

'Being lost is not funny. It's not funny at all. You can end up chopped up and what-not.'

That seemed to be all she had to say on the subject.

—

The image reflected itself on a mirror, which projected it through a lens installed up on the tallest point of the tower, and from there it reflected on the rotating white screen. With the help of a handle Raven wheeled the round screen to right and left, gathering in its curvature the whole of the town in an actual image, a perfect slice of life in movement.

With a long stick Portia followed one person or another from street to street, from the Pit Heads to the pub, until they got inside a door and disappeared. It was like being a bored God, sitting on the edge of a cloud.

Raven saw him then, the strawberry-blond boy, holding a brown paper parcel, going round a group of women gathered outside a butcher's shop. She saw him turn a corner. And she understood where he was heading, and hoped that Portia didn't see it, that her cousin decided on following somebody else. Raven then saw him stop, look right and left, and finally cross the alleyway, careful not to slip and fall with the puddles from recently fallen rain. He got there in the end—Barter's & Sons bookshop, a heave of insurgents and saboteurs.

'Well, well,' said Portia. Raven felt her cheeks burnt red-hot. She was worried Portia possessed any of the old family traits, long lost and gone. What if she could read minds, for example? She had never heard of anyone who could, but *what if*?

She herself had nothing, of course. No special traits. She was not like her mother had been. *The*

94

thing hadn't happened yet. She had to reach puberty, that's what everyone had said. Will she be able to perform spells to protect the strawberry-blond boy then? She didn't know. And she didn't have anyone to ask either.

Portia said nothing more, and closed the lens. The room collapsed into darkness.

———

They talked about many things. About music, about school, about television and books. It was easy to talk with Port about almost everything; everything but *the thing* and the strawberry-blond boy with glasses. She wished she could bring herself to mention any of them, but she couldn't, until one day it was Portia herself who did.

'I'll have to report him, you know.'

'What for? Going into a bookshop?' she found herself protesting.

'Everyone goes there for the same reason. They are all involved in it, or they end up being involved.'

'Then why don't *you* shut the bookshop?' she said, before she realised what she was saying.

'Hey, calm down... *You*? Who is *you*, anyway?' Portia said. 'I don't make the rules, okay? This is only my job. A job. That's it. But, do you want them to succeed? Do you want them to turn every Pit Head into ashes? What will we do then?'

Portia looked away. Raven wondered how much her cousin believed her own words. She was surprised that a girl with a Sex-Pistons t-shirt would say such things.

'I hate this town,' was all Raven could say at last.

'Yep, much better to be taken to another galaxy in one of the flying saucers that land in the meadow from time to time. That's what the stones are really for, didn't you know?'

Raven cracked with laughter. But she didn't know if Port was lying or not. She looked utterly serious.

The image was round and see-through, yellowish, as if she was looking into a cauldron of melted Ambar. Raven had never seen any Ambar, really, but knew it was a highly prized and beautiful substance, rocks with little insects inside.

She looked at the yellowish image, a man and a woman crossing town, and wondered if she would be fated to see always, always, life reflected over that white empty cauldron.

It was all her fault. She had left the meadow without looking where she was going, and as fast as she could. It had been too late to hide when she saw them, the strawberry-blond boy with glasses and the ash-blonde girl, elegant and beautiful and as out of place as an exotic flower. Two heads put together and talking in murmurs, conspiring. And barely a metre from where she was.

The boy looked at her, but this time his look was one of hatred. And then she knew it; he had heard, somehow, somewhere. He knew that her family was in charge of the Eye.

They got up and left, throwing disgusted glances back at her.

She wished a hole would open into the ground and swallow her whole.

This didn't happen.

She wished a door would open into another realm and absorb her.

This didn't happen.

She wished a gateway would appear in one of the stones, a huge mouth which would gobble her up.

This didn't happen either.

The stones were warm and soft to the touch. She had an odd sensation, and she understood why almost immediately. The light was wrong somehow. The stones reflected it, and the whole meadow seemed like the wrong meadow, a mirror image of her own. There was something off-putting, oddly untrue about the place.

But it was her meadow... Or was it? She wasn't sure anymore.

She got up, feeling warm inside, anger coming up her throat.

Raven felt something wetting her legs. She was bleeding, at last... But the notion brought no relief, no joy, no change in what she was feeling. Hatred. For the town and the Eye and the Pit Heads and the insurgents and the Iron Lady.

In front of her, at a distance, she saw the Northern Pit Head burst into flames, little ones this time, which were quickly extinguished.

Behind Raven the stone circle shone madly. Something had fluttered by her face, coming between her and the stones. It was a hummingbird, hovering over a small group of flowers, poised at a pitch-perfect forty-five degree angle, as if resting in midair. It was green and blue, with a golden shimmer all over its chin and breast, a red crown, wings coloured a deep indigo magenta.

This could not be. She knew her *Birds of the British Isles* sufficiently well to know that much.

She started walking downhill, wishing she could get lost. Behind her, light and shadows changed places in the meadow, but she didn't have a chance to see it.

———

There are many ways of getting lost.

One could fall into a deep ravine, or a mining pit.

Be taken into the sky by the gales that rolled over from the coast.

Absorbed into a cloud.

Kidnapped by aliens.

You could die, of course.

People died all the time; there was nothing strange in it. They had an accident, or they drowned, or they died because they were too old, or because they developed a disease that finished them in decades or in years or in months or in weeks. And then they were gone, from one day to the next, with shocking certainty, leaving a hollow space that nothing could ever fill. Their things disappeared next, the objects that made them the people they were. Their rooms got emptied, their clothes were dispatched to the Oxfam shop, the things they treasured—watch; tin box for rolled cigarettes; faded photograph of younger student days; a tiny bib from when Raven was born; the keys to a car that they didn't own anymore—were put in a carrier bag and buried, secretly, at the back of a teenager's wardrobe. And then their absence filled everything like a bad dream—only this wasn't a dream—covering everything like thick fog for a long while. Until, one day, the memories finally melted, and they fizzed out completely, a soft summer haze.

At the end, it was almost as if they had never existed.

They were spirited away, more forcefully than if aliens had taken them.

'Your uncle will be gone for a couple of weeks. We'll have to start sharing the shifts,' said Portia, sipping her beer.

The thing had finally happened. She was a 'woman' now, and this was a kind of celebration. It was Raven's first time in the *The Cog & Whistle*, but the waiter hadn't bothered to ask her age to serve her some soft cider with lemon. The problem had been of a different nature.

Before they entered, some men at the door had spit on the floor after Portia had pushed past them with her most sarcastic grin on her face. Once inside, Raven would have thought that everyone stared at them for a second, exactly like it happened in bad old movies.

'Don't pay attention, we are good customers here, exactly like them,' said her cousin, advancing towards the bar without worrying a second for anyone, as comfortable as a pig in a puddle of mud.

The Iron Lady shouted over a set of black microphones in the small television screen.

'I say, the woman is not real. She is a robot!' a young man shouted to no one in particular, stopping to stand next to Portia.

'Really, is that so?' she ventured, rolling her eyes at him.

This was enough incitement for the young man to sit down at their table.

'They say she is all wheels and cogs inside... No heart there, nothing human. Maggy the Doll!'

Portia smiled at him. Raven saw it then, the man motioning to his friends to join them, a punk with hair died yellow and black, and... Him. The strawberry-blond boy with glasses.

He looked at her intently. Raven could not stand that look, couldn't interpret it. She got up.

'I better go back home,' she said.

She reached the pub's door in a second, her heart racing wildly inside her chest.

———

When it happened it did not surprise her, at least not much.

She followed Portia with the lens for something to do, and saw her little reflection over the white pit of the camera obscura. She was getting used to working the Eye, to understand its power and the need for it. She felt as if she was passing to the 'dark zone', but that was the deal. Some kids went down into the pit age twelve, and Earth spit them out at the end of their first shift full grown men and women. Who knows what went on down there. More and more men and women were needed as the country's industry grew, and Great Britain struggled to become one of the Strongest Economies in the World on its own, outside of the world alliances it had proudly refused to join. And her role in the endless assembly lines of life was to work the handle, to turn the lens, to see what happened below. Accepting this was also growing up.

Port had met someone inside a café, but she couldn't see who she was having tea with in a little table by the window, so she pulled the handle with all her might and moved the structure into another area of the city to continue with her routine.

She saw her again by chance, later on, crossing the Main Street.

The blond boy was with her, and they were holding hands.

Of course, thought Raven.

———

It went like this: Portia would meet the blond boy in a café, they would walk together to the outskirts of the town, and then she would lose sight of them.

She knew exactly where they were heading; she had shown Portia her secret place herself.

'They are okay...' she had said about the stones. 'But if I were you I would be careful when I was up here.'

'Why? Because the aliens can kidnap me?' Raven tried a little laugh.

'The aliens? Well, this looks exactly like the kind of place where they would land, so I stand by that... But I mean something else. There is a force here...'

'I know. I can feel it too.'

They were both serious for a moment.

'Something is not okay up here, Raven. I am serious.'

She had been serious, it seems, about getting Raven away from the meadow, so she could take her boyfriend there!

She saw them disappear in that direction. To the only place unseen in the whole of the damn county. She wanted to scream.

Although she knew she shouldn't do it, she closed the lens and let the darkness wrap itself around her. She opened the door and started climbing down the stairs. She started thinking stupidly that it would be her birthday soon, as if that changed anything, meant anything. She suddenly realised something: her uncle's absences, Portia's coming from another town to instruct her in the use of the Eye... She would not go back to school that autumn. It was her time to go down into her own pit. And the sudden knowledge didn't hurt her, or upset her. It was only the truth, the reality.

It happened at that moment. She desired to see her mother again, and it was a feeling so strong and sudden that she feared she had invoked what happened. She was climbing down the stairs when she saw her. The corridor was bathed in the uncertain light of dusk. Outside, a light rain started to fall, leaking through the window that she could never close.

The shadow stood for one second at the corner of her eye. It was the shape that had convinced Raven she had been right: the thin tall figure, the pixie haircut, the white nightgown. That way of leaning against the threshold of the room.

She was certain, but it had been an unusual certainty, sensed more than actual. And she was so exhausted that the vision made no impression on her. It was a wasted moment of wonder, and later on she would ask herself how many more had passed her by like that.

Much later on she will remember it differently, the faded memory acquiring layers of consistency and relevance which each retelling.

—·—

When she reached the meadow the little rain had extinguished itself, and Port and the blond boy were lying on the wet grass, oblivious to any discomfort.

She didn't feel anything about what she was seeing. She had nothing left to feel. Their delicate movements, the little gestures of tenderness with each other, it all meant nothing. She wasn't happy or sad. But she thought... She thought... She wished...

It was the hummingbird again, appearing out of nowhere. And the soft yellow light bathing the stones, sending fantastical reflections from the quartz one, engulfing the meadow in an impossible circle of light and something different, something unreal. Light and shadow seemed to reverse for a second, as reality shifted. Raven saw everything, understanding it, deep inside, a knowledge brought by from somewhere, imparted by someone, oddly invisible.

It happened then, the door opening. Not to another galaxy, perhaps. But Portia and the blond boy absorbed that odd light inside themselves; and when it went out, they travelled along with it to the beyond.

The dark and grey sky hung again above the empty meadow. Portia and the blond boy were gone.

Raven stood up and turned to go back home.

Then she saw it: the four Pit Heads were shouting flames at the same time, engulfed in their ultimate destruction.

The government helicopters and drones were flying towards her valley, letting their own massive source of light fall from their bellies to obliterate it forever.

LOVE(GHOST)STORY

TODAY I'VE SEEN HIM AGAIN. WALKING UP AND DOWN the living room, shaving in the bathroom. Watering the plants, sitting by the chimney, absorbed in his book on Japanese botany. Tapping a ghostly tune with his fingers, just as he did while he was alive. The twilight brings him back. I lean against the door frame and I look at his face in the mirror, as methodical and concentrated on his task as always. He smiles back at me. He participates in my existence from his parallel plane, wherever that is: he can see me. This knowledge fills my heart with hatred. He turns towards me; he's going to say something. But he thinks better of it at the last minute, the words remaining, forever, unspoken.

He has resumed all his activities: pacing the entrance hall, the little balcony, the powder room, all the different chambers of his living days. I observe him interact with those who are oblivious of his departure—the maid who brings the tea and takes the dirty laundry, the new postman. He participates in their daily routines, walking up and down our lodgings with feigned happiness, filled with inexplicable purpose. He is forever about to say something, begin an activity, go out onto the little balcony, hang that picture we bought in Paris in another life, in that more solid world we once inhabited. But he always ends up repeating the same cycle: shaving, watering his favourite plant, the bleeding heart that leans out of the balcony. Then, he sits down with the same book, forever on the same page. Japan. Plants and trees. Aokigahara. The Sea of Trees.

I wait for him every twilight. We sit together. He smokes, reads, smiles.

We do not speak, really. What do you speak about with the dead? I don't think either of us minds the silence. I am thankful for the appearance of this shadow; this is the farthest I've walked from loneliness this winter. I wait for him; he waits for me. Last night, arriving at home later than usual, I was surprised to find him standing in the middle of the bedroom. No screams or fists banging on the bed; at least I'm free of that now. But his anger remains clear, justified. His disappointment. It's been curious to return to the cyclic repetition of our little dramas in this fragile universe... My head is spinning. It's the white of the snow, heavy with spectral reflections. Are we even still in London? I cannot recognize this street, covered with its pale shroud. The vision of the snow gets inside, to the room where I'm writing, making me shudder. It's the frosts, one day and another, the stillness of everything, the objects covered in dust, waiting for him. The eternal whiteness of a morning without shadows, of an evening with too many of them. Love, and its sweet—impossibly sweet—poison.

———

Dicentra Formosa: bleeding heart. The isoquinoline alkaloids are toxic to animals and humans. When consumed, it can produce liver damage, lethargy, palpitation, respiratory failure, seizures, cardiac paralysis, and ultimately death.

———

I don't go out anymore. I couldn't go anywhere without him. The house equals the universe.

I finally understand it all. I am his, forever; exactly as he said I'd be, once upon a time. Eternally. My means of escape was also how this prison was built: he is here, with me, forever.

So it is true, I say to myself. It is true. Nothing can compete with this, nothing at all; nothing can compare with the impossible love of the dead.

The Ravisher, The Thief

'Feel him. There's still a piece of him left,' her mother said, taking Paloma's hand and putting it to the back of her twin brother's neck. It was still warm. But Paloma held no illusions; he had already made the jump. What remained here was a carcass: empty, useless. His soul, his essence— whatever it was that made him who he was—was out there now, orbiting a distant star in a faraway universe, in a new home that wasn't dying as Earth was dying. If one chose to believe the parrot chants of the new believers. Here, now, to those who had cared for him, he was dead; they would have to bury him. So she prayed to the Raptors that he had made the jump safely, that she was wrong and he was right.

—⁃—

It had taken her two days to get there by foot, the lights of the city glimmering yellow and orange at her back during the one night of her journey. It was a steep climb, leaving the sea and up into the mountains.

The camp sat on a patch of brown grass which crunched under her feet. Inside their mother's tent it smelled of cooking, of the salvaged books and papers scattered around, of old fabric. The smells were mixed up with the hot, clammy air that entered through the open flap. 'Feel him', her mother had said as soon as Paloma entered, taking her hand.

Outside she could hear the birds, demented in their own tent, the kestrels, the merlins, the peregrines. She could feel their intense energy, her mind's eye sensitive to their nervous bating. Everyone knew the birds were psychic, and it was obvious to her that they had sensed her brother jumping. It was also obvious that the heresy had been too much to bear for the sacred creatures, for their displeasure was unusual; as if they did not understand, or as if they were mildly afraid. A silent and contained fear. None of their childlike, irritated shrieks. She could see it as clearly as if she were with them in their tent: the round eyes opened, the general panting and dishevelled feathers. Her own merlin had known something was wrong days before she had: his eyes shining wildly, his plumage tousled and on point. He had been unsettled even before she got word from her mother's commune kestrel.

And now another bird had sought her out here, bringing word from the Temple itself. She unrolled the parchment for the sake of her mother, always suspicious of her mind's connection to the birds, and read out loud the words she had already known she would find there.

'They need me back. There is an embassy coming and they need me to translate.'

The words hung in the air like an unwanted thing. She had no desire to stay a minute longer, and her mother knew it. Paloma felt as guilty as if she had conjured up the bird herself.

That evening she stepped out for a moment, and walked in the direction of the copse. She ended up standing among the eucalyptus trees. She didn't know what took her there, to the spot where they had enacted their endless religious arguments. Little routines are difficult to shake off, even at such times. She rolled her herbs, lit up and inhaled deeply. In her hand she was holding the vial where the poison, or cure, had been.

It was then that she saw him, in among the trees, his legs set slightly apart. One hand in the pocket of his jeans, the other bringing the smoke to his mouth and taking long slow drags, exactly as he did while he was here; exactly as he did while he was still alive, she could not help thinking. The twin brother she had abandoned to seek a better prospect.

Her brother's shadow turned to look at her.

It was only for one second, a moment out of time, out of reality, in which their eyes locked impossibly, either across the universe, as he hoped, or perhaps through a small rift between here and there, between life and death, like she feared. And which one of them was right?

Her brother's shadow flickered, and he was gone.

———

Paloma had never been summoned here before, and had never wanted to enter. The place was too much; it scared her slightly.

Among the rubble of the old civilization, the makeshift abodes, the new clay constructions, stood that monstrosity like an unwanted crown on the head of a reluctant king. The Temple was all that remained of one journey for her race that had come to a hasty end generations back. It had been called the Holy Family in those days, the *Sagrada Familia*, but no one knew to what family it might refer: probably some king or other, one of those few, far too few, who had owned the resources of the planet, sending the rest of the human flock down into a spiral of destruction. The building was impressive, some even said beautiful, despite its lack of avian ornamentation, but it spoke of a past world of fanciful constructions and wasteful artisanship. She had to gather her strength to set foot inside; her merlin had been left behind in her rooms, and without him she was feeling acutely exposed.

The Temple was now home to the Falconers. Around her many towers—more than ten surrounding the central one, a massive white cone shooting up as if it wanted to reach out as much as possible without flying—circled the many raptors that lived in the building: the merlin and the peregrine, the kestrel and the falcons: red-footed, lanner, barbary. She could also see some flying men, with their makeshift wings and their pince-nez, keeping an eye on the city.

'This way, please.'

She walked in. The inside of the Temple was vast and slightly confusing in its openness. She saw a forest of columns, all of them finishing in a profusion of what looked like carved palm leaves, all of them as high as it was possible to imagine, and judged that the builders had got it right: for a forest, of any kind, was the most sacred place on Earth, as it gave protection to all creatures. There were hundreds of people walking around, going diligently about their business or looking up in wonder: on first impression the Temple seemed a huge hollowed room, the reverse of the monstrous shape one could see from the outside. It appeared to have no chambers or corridors, no hidden alcoves. This, she would learn soon enough, was untrue, a deception created by the clever builders of the past. The noises of whistling and cajoling were deafening; everyone seemed to be manning a different bird.

The man-made sounds mixed with the chirping and the shrieking and the high notes of the birds. She followed the gazes of some people, overwhelmed by the immensity of the high ceilings, the concave arcs that sustained that fantasy miles up above her head, the capricious shapes that twisted and twisted, the curves, the angles, the fanciful working that kept those empty walls standing.

Were they really empty? It was true that they lacked any of the crude feathery drawings one was used to finding everywhere, and that their whiteness overwhelmed you for a second; but they had a profusion of carvings and little decorative holes and windows through which the birds flew to and fro, a constant fluttering of activity, of messages, orders, requests. It was mesmerising to watch. She had read somewhere that, long ago, those little openings had been covered with glass of different colours, and that the huge sections protected now by wood had been massive opened windows as well, also covered with translucent coloured glass. She imagined then the effect might have been dazzling, for she had also read that there used to be more light in the world back then, that their star shone more brightly, was not so used up. She found herself closing her eyes for a moment, trying to imagine 'light', huge beams of it crashing through the multicoloured glass, filling up that sacred vastness. It was impossible to picture, like looking at the signs of a language one is yet to learn.

'Please, follow me.' The usher was getting impatient, and Paloma wished they allowed a moment of reflection to everyone who entered the Temple for the first time.

'I've never set foot in here before,' she tried.

'Hmm,' was all the usher responded.

They ducked past a long line of dutiful young seminarians—all of them intent on carrying duty, a peregrine perched on their ceremonial gloves—got to a nave, and suddenly they were up one of the towers via some very narrow spiralling steps.

'You ought to be careful when you come back down; take it slowly or you may get dizzy,' the usher suggested.

Paloma thanked him, trying to keep up. Eventually they came to a recess, blocked off by a door which the usher knocked at lightly. It opened to an uncovered balcony-chamber, where a man in ceremonial robes was sitting at a table surrounded by kestrels of all sizes and colours, each perched on their own pole. She marvelled at their beauty, at their number, and could hardly mumble a greeting.

'Sister Paloma, it is a pleasure.'

'Father Merle, it's an honour,' she said, for she instantly knew who he was. He invited her to sit down and she did as she was told.

'I trust you got our summons.'

'I did. It didn't say...'

'Lake Baikal.'

'Oh!' Although she had expected as much. She knew several of the old commercial languages still in use, learnt from old books, sometimes tested, ever so slightly modified. She was capable, therefore, of understanding many embassies, but Old Rus' was in very high demand and she was one of the few who could still speak it.

Father Merle continued with what he was doing, imping the feathers' of a hawk's tail, carefully cutting and adding and repairing the weaker sections while the bird stood majestically still, her eyes and her head delicately turning, slowly, to the rhythm of Father Merle's soft whistling.

'This visit is of the utmost importance to us, Sister Paloma. You know very well how it has always been, since the beginning of our times. Whatever has come to pass...'

'Has happened first in the East.'

'Exactly. This Embassy could bring us cheerful tidings, or perhaps word of something... much darker.'

'The end of days?'

'It has been prophesied.'

She knew what he meant. Their religious belief claimed that the birds brought many kinds of messages, sometimes from other worlds, sometimes from a past where civilization had not yet dug its own tomb. She could feel her merlin alone in her room, across the large city, longing for her: the pull hurt deeply.

'I understand. I'm ready.'

'You will be allowed to carry your bird into the room where the talks are to be conducted, of course' he said, seemingly reading her mind.

'I thank you, Father.'

'Well, well. Ah!' Father Merle rewarded the hawk with a piece of raw meat, and whistled her back to her perch. It was beautifully done, and Paloma remembered the first three weeks with her merlin, all the tantrums and stubbornness the raptor had displayed. She belonged to the school of non-naming, out of some old-fashioned notion of not wanting to grow too fond of the animal. Like that had helped.

'The Embassy will land tomorrow at the port and will arrive here at the Temple one day later. Go back home, retrieve your bird and pack your belongings to stay here with us for a few days.'

'Thank you for this opportunity.'

'Not at all, not at all...' Father Merle was already up, turning to attend to his birds, and she knew herself dismissed.

———

There was a school of thought that insisted that the merlins ought to be allowed to fly free during the first few days of manning. The bird would come back a few times a day to feed. This only worked with the little birds that were still learning to fly, and she had not done it. It was a common occurrence that a small merlin had ended up being killed by bigger birds of prey, and she could not have endured it. The merlin was not her first bird, but it was the first bird of her new life in the city. She thought now of those first few nights, willing herself to keep awake, for the manning meant that the bird himself should not be allowed to go to sleep; consoling him after each bate, softly whistling, endearing. Annotating each morsel of meat eaten, each time he flew back to the ceremonial glove. The endless patience. The solitary days, the moment when he was introduced to other humans, once he recognised her and only her as his companion, his soul-tamer. The first longish flight and the first return, freed from the jesses. And the bates, and the stubbornness, for her merlin had been his own bird for as long as she could remember.

As soon as she entered she sensed that something was not quite as it should be. It was the silence, thick like a lie, hanging wetly on the room. Her merlin was nowhere to be seen. She preferred living in a clay dwelling rather than a tent, but it had little holes cut through the walls for the birds to come and go. She had never felt the need to cover them, for her bird had never disappeared. Not once.

Her heart missed a beat when she heard his recognisable fluttering and chirping coming from the larger hole, the one through which the Temple was visible in the distance, and she rushed there. The view over the city was of a grey mass of rubble, the distant Temple and the constant circling of raptors, so high up that some of them disappeared into the clouds, stepping into unreachable realms in their search for answers.

As soon as she was next to him, she knew her merlin was carrying a message. He had that look about him: piercing, suddenly alert.

'What is this?'

She unrolled the parchment.

The ravisher, the thief.

What could it possibly mean? The words had an odd flavour, of something heard long ago and forgotten. She left the parchment on the little wooden table and mechanically, still pondering its meaning, walked towards her clay snow-box, a luxury, where the precious meat was kept. She took out a rabbit's liver and walked back to the fluttering creature that was an extension of her own soul, which knew all of her deepest desires.

She could feel the bird's heart beating and started thinking at it: *where have you been, where have you come from, what are you telling me*, but the bird would not look at her. She presented the meat and he pecked at the liver with such force that he bit her finger, and she cried as if she were a young and inexperienced falconer:

'Robin, no!'

She was at a loss for a second as to why she had called the merlin by her brother's name.

Later on, she felt the known noise in the latch as it vibrated up and down. She got up to open the door. A six-year-old child entered the little chamber, and went directly to caress the merlin's beak.

'Branwen. Where is your mother?'

'In the Lesser Temple.'

Paloma sighed. Derora had developed a closeness to the new believers recently, to their empty promises. She had also started getting more and more silent and moody in the past few weeks, and Paloma had noticed she often left Branwen alone, when until not long ago she could not bear to be apart from the little boy.

'Have you eaten?'

She didn't wait for his answer, but went to the clay snow-box and retrieved the remaining meat.

'But... That's for him!' the child protested, unsure of how to react to her kindness.

'It doesn't matter, I'll buy more tomorrow. I've got myself some work,' she explained, already putting a little frying pan on the fire. 'But please don't tell anyone about the snow-box. It's a secret.'

After eating his fill the child fell happily asleep on her chair, and she carried him carefully to her bed-corner.

—⋅—

The meal consisted of rabbits, cats and turnips, a veritable feast. Paloma sat between one of the ambassador's secretaries and one of Father Merle's assistants. Each had a bird perched behind him.

Paloma brooded at her plate. She instinctively wanted to put aside the best bits for her raptor who, unlike other beasts, was used to cooked meat; she had to force herself repeatedly to remember that the food was for her own pleasure, that the raptors had as much as they could possibly need. There was no reason to exercise her natural economies while living in the Temple.

'You are not hungry?' asked the secretary.

'It's delicious,' she said, deliberately not answering the question. For she knew instantly what the problem was. She had been pecking at the sumptuous food all night, a meal she could have eaten only in her wildest dreams. She had not tasted cat in a long time, each acrid morsel as nutritious as the rest, and knew the meat came from a secret farm were the animals were reared for the very wealthy. She decided she would take some back for Branwen, if she could be careful enough not to be seen.

The reason for her darker mood was simple: the news had not been good. As a translator she was sworn to secrecy. She had been chosen because of her discreet nature. But the facts were alarming, and now she wondered whether she could cope with the pressure of knowing a truth that would remain hidden from the majority.

In the midst of the taiga, another hole had appeared, as black and menacing as all the others. But this one was different, so much so that news of its existence had to be taken to the Temple, the centre of the civilized world.

The birds that went into the hole never came out again.

They were used to their raptors moving between spheres, bringing messages and even in some cases small offerings: unknown plants, pieces of shiny fabric, things with actual colour on them, bright green, pink, yellow... This was the first time that one of the holes had opened into the true unknown.

The hole was slowly growing. It had been measured, and they kept an eye on it. Some thought this could be it, the blackness that had been prophesied, and that eventually it would swallow them up.

After dinner, Father Merle caught up with her in a round alcove.

'Sister Paloma. I ought to thank you personally: your translation skills are all we had hoped for.'

'Thank you, Father.'

'Pray, tell me, how did you learn Old Rus'?'

And she recounted again the story of her Father and her Mother, and their love for old books and papers and parchments, and their idea that most things could be found within them.

'As a result, we were always behind the other children in reading the signs of rain in the *tomillares*, or finding our way through the shrublands.'

They both laughed; Father Merle cut his laugh short.

'Sister Paloma, pray do not be offended by what I am about to say, for I do not doubt your professionalism, and your devotion to our belief...'

She frowned, unsure of where the older man was going with this.

'But, you see, I could not help noticing your look tonight. I just wanted to reassure you: there is no need to worry about what has been discussed in the Temple in these past few days.'

'But you said it yourself, the prophesy...'

He looked at her intently, as if judging something.

'I would like to show you something. Would you follow me?'

They climbed up the same spiralling steps she had taken on her first visit to the Temple, but went higher this time, up to a tiny landing that could only be situated at the very tip of the tower. He opened a door into a small room: no balconies, only one window and that boarded up. Oddly, not a single bird in sight.

'I was hoping you would not mind leaving your merlin outside for a moment.'

The request was odd, slightly tasteless, but she trusted him. She whistled a command, and the bird went to sit on a little perch outside the door.

'Thank you. And now, could I please ask you to sit here?'

He pointed at a chair in the middle of the room, where she sat. She lost sight of him for a moment as he walked over to a cabinet behind her.

'Please, Sister Paloma, I must request that you close your eyes.'

She sighed, unsure that she wanted to comply. But she was also curious. She took a second to sense her merlin outside: he was calm, collected. That convinced her there was no immediate danger, and slowly she let her lids fall over her eyes.

The dark, the hole in Siberia. Why did it all make her think of *him*?

A tear trickled down her cheek, and she was startled by its warm wetness. It was the first time she had cried over the loss of her twin brother.

'Open up, Sister.'

Her mouth opened as her eyes did, and slowly they moved around, as nervously as a bird's eye would, as she took in her new surroundings. The whole room had become a painted blackboard of the known universe, with stars close and distant shining in midair, and slowly turning and moving, a light spectacle like no other she had seen. Galaxies and supernovas and clouds of meteorites, in shining blue, projected above her by a beam of light that came from behind her.

'What... What *is* this?' she managed at last.

'This, Sister Paloma, is our future.'

'I don't understand...' But already the planets and the galaxies were zooming in and out, changing shape and direction, as Father Merle commanded the moving image directly to where he wanted to show her.

'AVA-2348, our final destination.'

Paloma shivered.

'How far away is it?' she managed to mumble.

'Our astronomers are still working it out. Several hundred light years.'

'But, how...?'

'Not all technology has been lost, and we've had help from our brothers and sisters of the past.'

Paloma turned to look at Father Merle.

'But I thought they were helping us to solve *this* mess...'

He smiled, ever so slightly, before saying: 'This *mess*, as you call it, has no solution, my dear.'

'But how are we going to get there?'

'I think you already know that.'

She didn't know what to say. Was it possible? Father Merle was one of the most powerful Falconers in Barna. Had he really gone to the other side? Had he really fallen for the sermons of the new believers? The preachings of a sect? It could not be true. She didn't want to believe it.

Then it hit her: this room was not difficult for the other priests to find. It was not hidden. She could not remember Father Merle even opening it with a key. Her whole body shivered at the implications: that they all knew, that they had already made a decision.

'Father Merle... What are you trying to tell me?'

'Our doctrine needs to change. We need to pass on the joyful message.'

'Joyful message?'

'There is a place beyond the stars so full of wonders, so beautiful, with so much life! And it is ours!'

'Ours?' Paloma could not believe her ears.

'Well, not *ours*, exactly. Only the courageous ones.'

'And what do they need to do, these people?'

'It's very simple, really. I'm sure you've heard about it.'

'Drink the potion?'

'That's exactly it!' He was smiling now, a wide fixed smile, as though he were a teacher and she a particularly apt pupil. 'I like you, Paloma. You are young, and clever, and a good believer. Here!' He handed her a vial. She held it in her hand, unsure of what to do with such a thing.

'I... Thank you, Father Merle,' she managed to mumble. She had sensed her raptor's nerves and was eager to get out.

'Sister Paloma!' he cried, as she was about to leave. 'Do you own a clay snow-box? For your bird's meat?'

She managed a nod.

'It is better to keep it there for the time being. Until you're ready, that is.' He smiled, and this time his lips were curving madly, and his eyes shone exactly like Robin's had, and she had to fight the tears, force them to hang a second longer by sheer will. 'It is very precious, you know.' he added.

'I will... Thank you, Father.'

Once she was outside the room, her merlin went to her arm and she found herself hurrying down the steps without looking back, down that same spiralling narrow staircase that ought to be taken slowly. The hurried descent eventually made her sick and dizzy, and she had to use one of its openings, high over the city, to let out a stream of vomit.

She was recovering when she felt it with a jolt: *The ravisher, the thief.* It was her brother the message had reminded her of. *The ravisher, the thief.* It sounded exactly like one of the things he would say in their endless religious arguments. *Look up their Latin name, would you?* he had said. *Did Mum and Dad teach you nothing?* The word she was meant to check was Raptor, of course. At those times, when he was more difficult to handle, when he was lost in his grandiose schemes and stopped making sense... At those times when she had not listened to him. Her mother had asked her back to visit, and she had not always gone. *The ravisher, the thief.* What had he been trying to tell her?

———

From her window she could see the city at her feet. Little yellow lights flickered here and there, and bigger fires looked like enormous circles of light, newborn stars around which other planets gravitated.

She wondered what would happen if she went to one of the fires and dropped the vial into it. Would there be an explosion? She was considering the damned thing, clasped in her hand, and it struck her how beautiful it looked; it seemed to contain all the colours she imagined the world ought to have, dancing in the viscous liquid.

She could not think. It was unbearably hot and her bird was getting uneasy. She left the vial inside the snow-box, put on her walking glove, whistled the merlin up onto it and they left her house.

They walked down to the sea together, the bird on her arm, only going for short flights to return hastily. Eventually they turned back and crossed the city again, the endless thoroughfares, straight lines dreamed by the architects of past days. Some constructions remained from those times, huge and ugly and covered in dirt and weeds and rubble. Standing on every possible corner there were people shouting their goods for barter and the continual aviary-related business, both legal and illegal.

They reached the beginning of the climb back to her mother's camp, and she had the sinking feeling that she would never go back there. She thought of the vial then, and started walking back home.

Merlin was starting to feel a tad heavy on her arm, too nervy, and she petted him for a bit. At last she whistled him to go for a longer fly; she thought he needed one. She continued walking, knowing that he would be back to find her later.

But he had decided to take his time, it seemed, and Paloma started to get worried.

At last she saw him; she could recognise him at a great distance, even in a sky heavy with dozens of birds. It was him, and her heart leaped a little; it was him, and he was carrying something back.

As her merlin approached her, he dropped his present at her, and she caught it in midair, that horrid offering.

It was the vial, and it was empty.

The bird fluttered madly around her; for she had not offered her gloved arm, and he wanted to rest on it. But what she thought for a moment was that he was trying to attack her. Heresy.

And then she thought of something else, another heresy, equally horrible.

Paloma started panting: the implications of this empty object, useless in her hand.

Who had found it? Who knew about her secret snow-box?

Branwen, answered her fluttering heart.

She set off running towards her house as fast as her legs would carry her, as fast as it was humanly possible to do so, wishing that she could fly instead.

Frozen Planet

BEHIND THAT DOOR EVIL LIVED. IT WAS THE SAME door, there was no doubt about it; Lawrence recognised the patterns on the wood and the little notches and ridges. The snow poured madly over its surface, pushing with all its force. He was going to try the handle, but he thought better of it. The same old fear came rushing in again, exactly as it had more than twenty years ago.

The door stood on its own in the middle of that white desert which moved with the intensity of the never-ending blizzard. It wasn't connected to anything; no wall or house supported it. It was perhaps the ghostly version of that same door... Or perhaps it simply *was* the same door, brought forward in time and space in order to torment him. It seemed solid enough. And behind that door, which had come out of nowhere, or so it seemed, his father was beating his mother. This was a fact, he was certain of it. He couldn't do a single thing. He just stayed there, unable to react, exactly as he used to do twenty years back, in another life, when he was a boy of twelve. He took a moment to rationalise the situation: they had been warned of this outcome, they had been prepped on the possibility of hallucination, mirages, fiercer in the snow than even in desert environments. Rigid, disorientating waves, formed by the winds over the snow, were called *sastrugi*. And the *nunatak*, an island of earth in the middle of the snow, always set at an unreal distance, another shadow.

He thought of an experiment: he started waking backwards slowly, careful not to trip and fall. The storm made progress a clumsy, indeterminate thing; he was sliding slowly backwards more than walking on his own two feet. Around him, there was only that constant hallucinatory whirlwind of dead white snowflakes, which made the simplest of tasks impossible, the white substance they hated so much forcing itself everywhere, obstructing his vision, filling his mouth with its sharp taste, numbing his face and his feet and his hands.

The door remained where it was. The savage weather made visibility ever more difficult until, after only five or six paces, he lost sight of it. But it was still there, he somehow knew it, with a certainty he could neither explain nor account for.

Then the howl came to him, taking him by surprise, ripping through reality without warning. It had been two days since they had heard it last.

The notion had been entertained, although with many reservations in some quarters, that the unseen beast had moved on, perhaps advancing deeper into the unexplored recesses of the unknown planet, leaving them able to snatch whatever rest they could inside their frozen tents.

And now there the howl came again, the beast making sure they did not forget about its existence. He felt lost, tired, he fought to prevent himself from vomiting on his useless feet.

———

They first heard it the day they went looking for Felix. They had managed to climb the left side of a little hill, near one of the valleys, following what looked like a ghostly path that he could somehow 'feel' existed under the snow shroud. They were all holding a rope in order to stay together, perhaps the only inhabitants of that vast white desert. The planet seemed to him then an infinite ocean of silence and absences.

All of a sudden the path became wider, opening into an unexpected avenue delimited by large boulders of ice balancing over their heads on either side. Some of them were enormous, vast and austere like out-of-place colossi, built by some god so at least one thing was made in His image, and was equally terrible.

They established the unexpected proportions of the avenue; they were off-key, everything too large, disproportionate, according to the information they possessed about the creatures that had lived on the planet. Simon reflected out loud that it looked like a thoroughfare, made by alien hands, perhaps in use when the planet had been inhabited. The elements, or time, or whichever form of destruction the place had endured, had covered the main access they had taken, and now there was no other possibility than to climb on foot as they had just done, as John assured them he had seen Felix doing the previous day.

Very early on during the ascent they had stopped seeing their tents, the broken exploratory vehicle abandoned farther beyond, and they felt stupidly lost then, as if the sight of those few elements of safety, of 'home'—a couple of rotten tents and a useless machine, which could hardly provide shelter for the whole group—meant something, the difference between life and death. But every inch they climbed left a taste in their mouths of leaving behind what stood in for them as the basis of the 'civilised' world.

The notion of the vast empty landscape overtook Lawrence, who felt all of a sudden even lonelier up here. It was a desolate feeling, imposed by the wind cutting your skin, the snow, sticky and piling on your eyelashes, the increasing and unbearable coldness, a warning implicit in its deliberate discomfort: turn back, it is your soul that is freezing. If you continue climbing this mountain, it will be death who you meet, it is life that you are leaving behind, do not be mistaken.

The crevices and the cliffs did not take long to appear, the uneven slopes, the frozen rocks and small stones which only the inexperienced eye dismisses as harmless, unaware that the tiniest of them can twist your ankle. You are stranded then, slowly or rapidly covered in snow, with only the company of those sad ghosts we all carry; a small stone all it takes to finish you.

Once on the summit of the hill, the dangers were different. They were conscious of the possibility that, before they found traces of Felix, some sort of avalanche would wipe them from its surface. They walked as slowly as they could, a line of mice in the middle of the blizzard, measuring every step, communicating with signs. Each and every one of the marks left by their boots was wiped out by the elements in less than a second.

Lawrence looked behind to reassure himself of the exit route. What he saw depressed him: there was nothing there, not even the tents below, or the small ship. They would stay stranded and lost in the middle of nowhere.

The blizzard gained momentum. It was very bad news indeed. To get lost in this part of the planet, almost unexplored and mostly uncharted, with barrows and crevices and openings everywhere leading towards some unknown and frightful abyss, would be deadly.

—

The chasms weren't the only danger. Just when they reached the middle of the thoroughfare something entirely unexpected happened.

The lives of these men were directed by precision, by protocols and rituals that could mean the difference between life and death. The hostile environments they had charted in their expeditions forced them to somehow reestablish priorities around survival lines: food, orientation, shelter. Their lives did not have space for superstition.

They continued advancing, painfully slow, against the wall of the wind. John had started signalling that they should head back, but Simon would not hear of it. His stubbornness had placed them in that situation in the first place, but the old bonds of loyalty were difficult to ignore. Lawrence, turning in Simon's direction, advanced towards the expedition leader, deliberately ignoring the pleas of the younger man. He was perhaps choosing death with that simple gesture; it remained to be seen. Further on there was the glacier, which they had baptised the Ocean of Ice, in memory of the one on the original planet of their forebears. They were heading towards it when it happened.

It was the dogs who warned them; their fearful whimpering seemed to announce that the devil himself was waiting for them behind the soft wall of snow, only an inch from where they were, but so hidden that it felt a league away. The animals started to struggle to turn round, suddenly incapable of moving, too strong-headed in their determination not to continue. They were crying, snarling. Simon started hitting them and shouting at them. The vision of the struggle, man against dog, dog against something, whatever it was, made Lawrence shiver even more. A shudder climbed his spine and prickled at the frozen hairs at the back of his neck.

Lawrence knew perfectly well, as did Simon, as did everyone else, that if the dogs left they were as good as dead. It would be impossible to get back to the tents, and they would surely remain stranded there, with even less hope than they had now. It was not all lost yet. Simon had assured them that the distress signal had reached its destination, and he believed in Simon. But they would not be found there, on that hill. The snow would cover them fast, and they would become another barrow, part of the hellish landscape of the alien planet.

—————

It was soon clear that the dogs' wailing was directed at something specific, a kind of indeterminate shadow which gained consistency with each advancing step, until it resembled a longish shape, a human form seen through the wall of falling snow. Someone was waiting for them in that godforsaken place. Felix, obviously. Even if the proportions did not match the figure of their friend, it had to be him.

Lawrence broke into a run, or tried to do so, only to find in front of them a softer spot of snow. Their legs and their boots sank deep into the white, making walking, or even moving, impossible. He managed to reach the shadow with the human form, but he also tumbled down when he got next to it, and it was only with great difficulty that he managed to stand up. He fell again. He looked up: there was nothing there. He shouted Felix's name, now on all fours, trying in vain to find a place to support himself and stand up once more.

It was then that he heard the squeal of a door opening, an auditory hallucination, completely out of place, which provoked an unease he recognised, a bitter feeling long forgotten which he could not place.

It was in this position that he found Felix's altimeter, sunk deep into the snow. There was no doubt it was his friend's; they both had the same old-fashioned model, and it had his initials engraved on it: F.J.W., Felix-Julius Walton.

They were all shouting in his direction. The blizzard had increased out of all proportion, magnificent in its death wish. They had to get back. The hill had become, according to the team's own vernacular, an 'easy spot to die in'.

———

They heard the howl for the first time, the desperate cry of some creature, something that had to be enormous and powerful, as big as a whale to make itself heard through that rattle of weather, making the very hills shudder, bringing a shiver to their human hearts.

———

There is talk amongst the men about what happened up on the hill. Nobody wants to be the first one to say it, that elusive word: 'apparition'. 'Ghost'. When Simon catches someone talking about it, he cuts it off root and branch; he does not approve of wasting energy on this kind of useless talk. Time passes, or so they think. Forty human hours, a long and exhausting day. To keep their energy, they mostly sleep. They usually wake up from a dark and empty sleep—the end of a tunnel, a well. There are no dreams; they would imply spending energy they do not possess, the very energy they need to crawl out of the sleeping bags, heat up some water, drink it, divide the nutrients, fall asleep once more, live a few more hours. Wait for the creature's growl. The historian explains that at home existed cultures that used to measure time in dreams instead of days. But there are no dreams here, and this is perhaps good. They would be tainted with the howls of the creature; they would be nightmares instead of dreams. All they have is the water, the division of nutrients to pour into it, and that dark stupor of not being able to count the days, or the nights.

And the chaos of the tent, infinitesimal shelter whenever a storm hits them.

———

The chaos outside is different. The chaos outside is death. White horror. Disorientation. To perish a few metres from the tent, a few metres from the frozen sleeping bag, and the water, and the out-of-date, perfectly preserved biscuits.

What you miss then is the inertia of those first few weeks of the expedition, on the southern side of the planet, the steppe long and unmoving, metallic blue, sandal pink, violet. Snow seemed never to be white there, on those far-off southern slopes; and when it was they had to come out of their tents to observe the marvellous absence of colours, the weird phenomenon that contradicted what they had learnt to believe, day after day. The world was the same unchanging vision, eternal, the steppe repeated into infinity. It was a different time, before the exploratory vehicle got broken, before they perished. Perhaps, he thinks, they have perished already, they simply are not aware of the fact. They are kept busy counting the forty hours they think make a day, boiling the water, counting the biscuits.

A conversation starts about those coloured steppes, a distraction from the beast. Some of the men in the expedition have been lucky enough to have known the oceans at home; they talk about the intense emerald green, the tired browns, all of them tinted by the olive hue of memory. They try to explain it to the younger men, but it is impossible to put into words. The ocean needs to be seen.

They discuss the journeys that got them there, the different circumstances that led each of them to volunteer. They do not discuss the journey back, or any possible rescue. The journey back is a different space, distinctively felt as another, carefully cut away from their existence on the metallic blue, pink and violet planet. As for the beast, it is prohibited territory. The world is a single panorama, eternal, broken only by the spectacle of the aurora, by the halos surrounding the four moons, by the clouds, as shiny as huge old-fashioned orange serving plates.

———

The world is also the storms, deadly, that come and go capriciously; wind blowing, stiffened extremities, the tons of solid clouds hanging over their heads, the snow, the snow, the snow.

The overpowering shadows, the dark reflections crossing the mountain planes, the ghosts and ghouls, the low clouds that play with your mind; a feeble sea, coming and going, never reached; a mirage, a phantasmagoria, a lying shadow. *Sastrugi, nunatak.* Borrowed words from a planet that doesn't exist any longer. One believes in mirages because there are no dreams, and one must believe in something.

———

And then there is the door, green paint licking the wood, the well-known ridges.

Felix.

He mentioned hearing the howl, before anybody else did.

He mentioned the hellish growl of something enormous, disproportionate, gigantic, a creature as big as a mountain.

He went to it, now Lawrence understands.

He mentioned the creature.

He also mentioned seeing his wife, that morning, outside of the tent. He saw her. Spoke to her. No one believed him, of course. Mirages.

In a second the mirage dissolves, and all is clear: Felix simply decided to go back home.

It was time Felix gave them, the greatest of all gifts. His sacrifice did not go unheeded by the beast, the god-like creature. After it had taken place the signal worked at last, salvation. Simon had assured

them it had reached its destiny, and he believed in
Simon.

—•—

There is hardly any mist, and the snow, dusty and
thin now, is no more than a yellow stain which has
decided to cover this piece of solid ice, twirling
around their legs, forming curves refracted over
the wavy surface, ever-changing but eternally itself,
forever itself, until the end of time. 'I am going out,
and may be some time.'

Lawrence goes out into the blizzard and heads on
in the direction of the howling.

The door is there, waiting for him, when he exits
the tent.

It has the same exact patterns on the wood and
the little notches and ridges. And behind it, he knows
it only too well, his father is beating his mother.

He takes the handle and turns it, opens the door
and crosses its threshold never to come back, never
to be found, towards the blizzard, towards the beast,
towards the unknown.

—•—

When the rescue team arrives on the planet the next
morning, he will be declared officially lost while on
duty.

MARVELS DO NOT OFTIMES OCCUR

The celestial phenomenon was duly recorded in manuscript, ballads, woodcuts, to be told and retold.

WE KNEW NOT WHENCE THEY CAME, NOR WHY THEY did as they did, but the ships in the clouds threw their rays onto the churches first. The towers got fire, and the bells tolled until they crumbled to nothingness. The lightning burnt first the Cathedral of Our Lady of the Penances, which blazed for two days and two nights before it was consumed. Died in trying to extinguish the fire: Jan Eikelaar, Samuel Rochestein, Adolf Steinmuller, Saint Valerian's day, April 14, 1561, sunrise, just before early mass.

Two kinds of vessel, the large and the small, swarming in a bloodied sky. They shone of their own light, both dark and bright blue, deep red. With them came a golden gloom, then all was covered by clouds. Rays. Mirages. They vanished to leave the vessels space for their parade. The sun blazed white, yellow, darkening to a sickly green, gliding and soaring and dancing in concord. After some time—it was but eight of the clock—a largest vessel appeared. It was black as pitch, a triangular shape of shadows, a triptych of wonder and awe and dreams.

Children ran into the streets, women went out of their balconies, men climbed to the rooftops, marvelled at the occurrence, a sign from the heavens, a day of feast. The little sparrows and doves flew drawing spirals, until they disappeared as well. They would not return for a week.

The vessels stayed in the sky for several hours, dancing. Then, of nowhere, giving no announcement of what act they would perform, they began to call down light and heat to the city, to burn the churches. All the townsfolk ran into their houses and when the tall was made after the destruction, all were found to be present, save two, to wit: Goodwife Anna Freytag and Hannes Kirkhofer. What is become of them I know not, may they be saved and protected.

For all that we have suffered, and have deserved to suffer, may God grant us his help. I put my hand to this true account, at Nuremberg, the third anniversary of the death of Doctor Johannes Bugenhagen of Wollin. What would he have made of it I wonder.

Kingfisher

While Birds of Calm sit brooding on the charmèd wave.
John Milton

I.

By the time we arrived we were so tired we couldn't unpack anything apart from the bird guides. They were too precious to spoil by leaving them longer than necessary in a suitcase filled with old notebooks and dirty underwear. Once we reassured ourselves that they had survived the long train journey, we sat on the couch still wearing our coats, and waited for darkness to fall around us. The dark was always very sudden here, like in the Tulgeywood. Eventually we dragged ourselves upstairs, undressed, and got into bed. We immediately recognized the cold and damp in the sheets. It was great to be home.

We had come back because of me. I could not write in the South, all those beaches and that white light everywhere. It was all too placid, too easy. Jonas had written a couple of good poems, but I was getting restless. I had sat by the window inspecting the sky with my binoculars: people said that sometimes you could still spot a kingfisher in this part of the world; the sightings were getting rare. I had read the guides, traced with my fingers the bright plumage in the illustrations, and scribbled in my notebook. Every evening we went out into the one long street that crossed the village. It was tuna season, and each bar offered their personal take on how to prepare it. They gave it for free, in small portions, whenever you bought a short glass of yellow beer. There were too many fish in the ocean, too little of everything else. I had not seen a dog in years, and had never seen a cat in real life. Some days those free tuna dishes were the only food we got to eat all day.

I was getting bored by then. Of the friendly faces, the easiness of it all. I started fantasising that I needed to deal with some obstacles in order to produce good material. That I needed to be a little bit uncomfortable, a little bit cold, a little bit unhappy. An excuse as good or as bad as any other, designed to clear my mind of the real fear: that I would never write again. My fellow classmates from the writing class I had attended were doing very well for themselves; some were doing incredibly well for themselves. I was ashamed of how jealous this made me: until then I had always thought I was a good person.

We had finally decided to come back for good one morning after a surprisingly bad fight. The change of scenery did not seem to have muted our problems. The locals celebrated one particular day in mid-July by taking the statues of the Virgin from the churches, placing them in beautifully decorated boats with flowers, candles, fruit and other offerings, and taking them out to the sea. It was an act of thanks, as it was said that the Virgin had stopped the town from flooding a couple of centuries back. We had watched it all from the beach one late afternoon, eating local tuna, and drinking the pale, yellow beer. The statue rocked left and right on the little boat, precariously advancing over the deep. A little flotilla of other boats escorted her. On the blue, shiny sea, a prevalent Sun descended, turning the sky an ominous purple. Soon all that could be seen were little candles, flickering here and there, lost at the far end of the ocean. After the procession was over, we went back to the apartment we were renting and had a fight about our ancient grievances. The next morning we woke up to the news a fisherman had killed his family during the night. I did not want to pursue the gruesome details; I did not want to know, so I never got to hear how many people he had killed, or why. Later on there was speculation that the big tuna had been contaminated with pesticide, Lindane or something similar. Some people had reported hallucinations: seeing visions and hearing voices. We decided to leave the following week.

Money was a constant conversation everywhere. The fisherman had been heavily in debt, and he and his family had been about to be evicted from their house. We panicked a little. Jonas and I had been discussing for a while that perhaps one of us should try to find regular employment. We talked about whether we could stay and do that in the little village, but figured it would have been impossible to earn a living there: after years of expensive academic education, we had absolutely no practical skills. Sometimes it felt as if all the sacrifices that my parents had made to provide me with a better future had been for nothing. Thinking about it made my stomach twist unpleasantly.

As soon as we returned home we fell into the usual routines. Jonas had his own parallel existence. It involved witty friends scattered over an array of social media platforms, his books, and the poems he never let me read until they were published somewhere, as if my possible contribution to a work in progress might taint them somehow. The evenings were particularly lonely. He read very fast, and could be on a new book every time we sat together on the sofa, but he never shared anything with me, never talked to me about what he was reading that day or why. He only looked up from his book when there was a beep in his little social media pager, indicating a reply to something he had posted. I watched series reruns, and felt guilty for not writing, but could not have started a conversation with him about the topic. I knew what his answer would be: that if I wanted to write all I had to do was to switch off the old television set, sit down at the dining table, and put pen to paper. So I said nothing, and he said nothing. It was frightening how comforting was to fall back into the known, mute dynamics. We had discovered some damp on one of the sitting room walls when we got back, and choosing the wallpaper, putting it in place, and generally treating the damaged area kept us busy and gave us something to discuss. We were really good at this, finding little projects that meant we did not need to talk to each other about anything meaningful or possibly upsetting. The paper was beautiful, with green parakeets, a very rare thing.

It wasn't long till I got a job in a library. I filled in the application form in the breaks from putting up the beautiful parakeet wallpaper. Years earlier, when I was still deluding myself that I could be an academic, I had left behind a really good job in a library. The job had started as something to keep me in funds as a student. At about this time I met Jonas. He had a full scholarship and I didn't, so I worked in libraries throughout my higher education, but it turned out I was good at it. Would I like to become a librarian? The library would pay for my librarianship degree, on the sole condition that I came back to work for them for three or four years after graduating. I went as far as attending the interview in London and being accepted in the program, only to decide at the last minute that I didn't want to be a librarian after all. So I stopped working in libraries. A few months after that we started our wandering years as freelancers. We did everything: we wrote articles, did translations from three or four languages into another three or four languages. We ran a little printing press, producing books from our kitchen table, which at the best of times gave us enough money to live. But one of us had needed a job, and so I got one.

The work felt completely new and strangely familiar, as if I had found, after years of abandoning it, an old coat forgotten in a wardrobe. It still fitted me perfectly, and it was the most comfortable thing in the world. I had a regular salary for the first time in years: on the thirty first of each month money would appear in our joint account as if by ma. I could finally put behind me the years of waking up at two or three in the morning, filled with anxieties relating to money and freelance work. Sometimes we had been paid, sometimes we had not been. Jonas worked very hard as a translator, but despite his efforts it wasn't enough to give us financial stability. His father, a well-known ornithologist, got him work sometimes translating bird guides. There had been a couple of particularly miserable years, with translation work slowly eating us up, the little press doing as well as it would, and both of us slowly accepting that none of this was enough to keep us going in the basics of food, clothes, shelter. The change from that to being paid regularly was like taking a draught: I could sleep soundly again. Things were looking up, we thought. Things could in fact only get better. One of us having a job was a better prospect than anything.

Perhaps this was how things stood now. The world seemed to be compressing somehow. Possibilities that had been obvious to our parents even one generation back were now impossible dreams. Housing was unaffordable, so we would never own a place of our own, although at the same time there were hundreds, thousands, of houses and rooms empty up and down the country. They were just owned by other people, not us: banks and companies and trusts and corporations. After finishing our shiny and expensive educations, we hung the orotund Latin certificates and proceeded to fail, industriously, in finding the jobs that we had been promised. Jonas always made fun of me for wanting to hang the certificates, and insisted on our doing so in the bathroom, directly over the loo. Whenever I was lying in the bathtub, I could read the luxurious cream-coloured pieces of paper, stating that in the register of such and such institution it appeared to say that... The wording unnerved me so. There were not many cars anymore, no air travel, although I was secretly happy about this. I remember flying once, when I was very little, how frightening it was, how miraculous it felt. But the wrong kind of miracle, like black magic. The plane was a blue, impossible metal bird. I was terrified, the whole notion was terrifying, climbing up thousands of miles up in the air locked up in that little tin contraption. A nice man saw I was frightened, and explained to me that I didn't need to fear, that it was like when a boat goes on water. I didn't believe him, of course.

But there was more: a great number of animals had disappeared with speedy finality from the face of the earth; everyone seem to have difficult pregnancies and problems conceiving, and so every year fewer children were born. This brave new world was about wanting fewer things, not more things. There were no more certainties. But I did not see why I could not work in a library, and write stories, and translate books, and keep our little press running. I didn't see why I needed to renounce even one of these things.

I also wanted, more than anything, to keep little birds in a huge cage shaped like a palace. But that particular desire was surely nothing more than an impossible dream. I did own a huge cage shaped like a palace, an antique. It was empty.

When I was student I had read about a famous American poet who had also wanted to do more than one thing. But to her, wanting everything had not left her paralysed like it had me: she became a famous poet after all. She had also ended up with her head inside an oven, but even so she had not been gobbled up by history, as had happened to so many women who had managed to do even one of the things they wanted to do. The American poet had kept bees. It took me a long time to find out what bees were.

I had also wanted to have a child at some point. We had been younger and not aware of the general difficulties, and Jonas and I had managed to at least conceive on a few occasions. By the time we had stopped trying to become parents, a year and a half after my first miscarriage, I had stopped counting how many pregnancies I had lost. Now I wasn't so ambitious, not really. Air travel? Bees? A child? Not anymore. All I wanted was to see a kingfisher, only once.

2.

Sometimes there was a vintage clothes fair in the town hall. A lady who sold furs went there. They were old, at least third hand, probably fake, but I loved touching them. Would it feel like that to pet a little cat, a rabbit? I had no idea what a rabbit looked like, but the notion of them, and of hares as well, scared me a great deal. Until adulthood I had thought that rabbits and hares were as big as men, and that horses were little. Apparently I had seen a picture book about something called ponies very early on, and had mistakenly thought that all horses were like that. I had never sought out pictures of people on horseback, so the first time that I stumbled upon one in a book, I had a strange sense of void, as if the world didn't make sense somehow, or I had missed something relevant. Those animals were enormous, monstrous things. I looked hard at the black and white picture. I remember I was working in one of my first libraries, so I was hiding between the aisles, looking at the books I was meant to be reshelving. The people on the horses were obviously adults, and definitely not small, but of average stature. I almost fainted.

I had also thought for most of my life that seahorses weren't real, and when Jonas explained to me that they had really existed I laughed at him. I had thought they were mythological creatures, like fairies or unicorns. No, unicorns had apparently existed as well, he claimed. But I knew he was wrong. He was just too arrogant to admit it.

What I had longed for, and for some time now, was to see a kingfisher. I had collected over the years a few precious pictures and every bird guide that came my way, and I knew well the bright plumage of so many different shades, the bird's determined chin. I thought it the most beautiful bird in the world. We had travelled South because it was common knowledge that there were more birds there. The abundance of sea creatures meant that many birds were happier living close to the ocean, in order to have something to eat. But I had other reasons to want to go near water to see one. I had read that kingfishers made a little nest on the ocean's surface to lay their eggs: a nest of little twigs and bones. When they did this, the waters calmed, and sailors could go safely about their chores.

I had never yet seen a kingfisher alive, but I had managed to see a stuffed specimen in an ethnographical museum. Apparently, the exhibit was an amulet designed specially for that purpose: safe sea travel. When animals started dying in great numbers, a taxidermological frenzy had begun, and now the very wealthy owned their own dusty menageries, frozen in time. Some museums also contained similar specimens. I had made an exception that day and sought out the kingfisher: I normally tried to avoid stuffed animals. Their moth-eaten faces depressed me.

I was sitting one day in my office in the library when I saw a strange yellow light coming from underneath the door. I set aside the Italian book I was trying to catalogue, got up and went to open the door. The library was not there, and I found myself in a garden. It was man-made, formal, more French and Spanish than English; some yellow sanded paths around mouldy statues and fountains whitened by a flat, oppressive light. I advanced slowly through it, trying to locate where I was. The trees and the flowers were tropical, but I suddenly knew that I was in England. I walked around it, and came to the end, or rather to the boundary where the formal garden mixed with a profusion of greenery that seemed to have gobbled everything up, as jungle and town mixed. I could still recognize some of the buildings: the glass dome of the History faculty, the high tower of the big academic library all the other little libraries pledge allegiance to. I orientated myself, and got as far as the river, and a little bridge between two colleges. I could see the huge back garden of King's, but all was covered in the same white oppressive light, and the banks of the river were scattered with palm trees and lianas falling on the water. I could see strange things flying around, but no birds, sadly; they looked rather like insects, huge flying ants and beetles, making a persistent humming noise.

Another strange sound startled me. I had never heard it before, but somehow I knew they were parrots. My heart soared.

Then there appeared a little flock of hummingbirds, blue and pink and yellow and beautiful. They were playful and tame, and came very close to where I was standing on the bridge. They seemed curious of me; I could extend my hand very slowly, and they would let themselves been touched. And they were as soft and furry as the coats on their moth-proof hangers.

Suddenly I felt the strange void again, as had happened when I saw the photograph of the horses: I knew it to be unnatural to be surrounded by those birds there, at that moment, those birds lost to the world a whole century back. They had been a symbol of all that was lost, and it had become fashionable to have tattoos of hummingbirds for a while; people thought they could keep them forever like that. They were the most reproduced, tattooed and painted birds in history, so there was no possible confusion.

I woke up with that anxiety of nightmares, even though the dream had been so beautiful until that last moment of strange recognition.

I left our bed as quietly as possible and went downstairs. The living room was warmer than the bedrooms, but I still had to wrap myself in a blanket. I made coffee, sat down at the dining table, and started writing a story for the first time in months.

I should have known even then that the act of writing was beyond me. I felt as if I would let go of it, slowly at first, and then suddenly, irrevocably. Like when you grab some sand in your hand on the beach and let a few grains fall. And then a few more, until it becomes impossible to resist opening your fingers. In the end you yourself let it all go, quite willingly it seems.

It was something very little at the beginning. A book left on the floor next to the bed. A jumper that one day ended up on the sofa and proceeded to be never put away. A muddy glove that had fallen to the ground when entering the house, and had been left there.

It was the glove, in particular, that sent me over the edge. Every morning I would leave for work, thinking that it would be eventually collected and put out to be washed. That turned into a hope every morning that today would be the day when it finally wouldn't be there when I came back. And that turned into the stubbornness of telling myself that I would not be the one removing it.

Jonas had always enjoyed cooking, and that had become his usual activity, with the implication that I was in charge of the cleaning. In the past I had also enjoyed cooking as well; but at least by accepting this arrangement my mind could be free from one tiresome household matter. Jonas was better at cooking at me, more imaginative, and he fed us well, even at the scarcest of times; but the kitchen after his ministrations looked like a war zone.

I started avoiding the kitchen. It was so depressing; it made me so angry. I did not want to have more fights with Jonas. I think that my avoidance of the kitchen upset him; he never thought it was fair I did not help more with the food. But after so many years of the arrangement I could not go back: it was clear that, if I started accepting more responsibility in the cooking, Jonas would creep out of it and reclaim more time for his favourite activity, reading. He always made the preparations in a little corner on the counter, and things fell on the floor there: potato peelings, bits of bread, sprinkled flour. This debris would just sit there, on the floor, for days on end, sometimes weeks.

One day he surprised me with a delicious meal: tuna steak, lightly fried, marinated in soy source, and with some little potatoes and greenery from our garden. Apparently, it was the same kind of fish we had eaten in the South, brought over to England by the huge freezer boats that caught it. It was delicious, just like tasting the light. Every evening I would get back and collapse on the sofa, and watch more reruns of TV series. I would then look at the table where my story sat, scribbled in old pieces of reclaimed paper. I blamed myself for being tired. I had ideas for many stories, stories about floodings, and about snowed-in places about to become flooded. Stories about birds and strange flowers. Stories about glaciers and jungles and strange weather and lost things. Stories about ghosts and forests and wolves in sheepskin. I looked at the table and longed not to be so tired, not to write so little. We fought often, but I could not have explained what the fights were about. I seemed to have a very selective memory for those things, or perhaps I could not face the consequences of the fighting, and forgot it all with real ease.

About that time my boss had been getting fatter and fatter, until one day she revealed the truth: she was expecting what she said was a child, and would leave the library shortly after. I did not know what to do with that revelation, precious as a rare bird. I gained extra responsibilities. Now, each twenty-sixth of the month we woke up to even more money in our joint account. Jonas celebrated by buying more books to read. I had not read anything in weeks. I would wake at six in the morning, but never managed to leave my bed immediately. I went down to make myself some coffee, and by the time I was sitting at the table I only had one hour before needing to get ready for work. I was managing very little, at tortoise speed. I cycled to the library and worked until five or seven in the evening. I then cycled back home; collapsed; ate something Jonas had prepared for us—tuna fillets, clams in *pimentón*, bread surprise, mock crab; went up to bed; fell asleep, woke up and started it all again. Eventually I admitted defeat: I was achieving so little waking up that early that it was almost not worthwhile, and it left me exhausted during the rest of the day.

I started to have strange dreams at that point. They mostly involved being trapped in small places, cupboards, rooms. In a strangely elaborated one, I had to scuba dive along an underground tunnel filled with water, its walls the immaculate white of old-fashioned space travel movies, to emerge in a subterranean world where the most varied fauna roamed free. I understood in the logic of the dream that once you came out of the tunnel it meant that you were living in some kind of virtual reality, while your body was kept in suspended animation above ground. It did not matter, this virtual and unreal world was full of wonders: zoos, safari parks. Birds were flying everywhere. I saw hundreds, thousands of them, flocks forming curious shapes in mid-air. I spent the whole dream reminding myself that

I needed to ask someone about the kingfishers. Were there any? Where to go to find them? But, equally, I spent the whole dream failing to do so, or incapable for some reason. Eventually, it was time to come back, or to wake up, within the dream, and I had to scuba dive again along the same white and narrow flooded corridor into the 'real' world. I woke up with a strange feeling of dread, limbs so heavy I imagined for a second I was trapped somewhere, with no space to move. Only gradually was I capable of moving again, of ascertaining that I was not in the 'real' world of the dream, but in the 'real-real' world, two stages above, and that therefore everything was fine; it had to be fine.

Except that there were no zebras or swans here, two of the animals I had just seen. To my disappointment I had not been able to touch them, and I had only been able to look at them from a safe distance. Someone in the dream had explained: they looked like beautiful animals, idyllic and majestic. But the zebra could kill you with an expert kick if she got angry, and swans weren't as fluffy as I had imagined. They could apparently break a man's arm with a single blow of their wings.

It took no little effort to admit defeat and change my routine. My new plan was to write at night. It would take all my will power not to succumb to the series reruns. The previous year I had watched the life of a mother and a daughter who lived in a quaint little town. The series took years, from the moment they moved to the town to when the daughter finishes university. This year the rerun was about a girl who killed vampires and zombies helped by a librarian. The series reruns took a lot of commitment, as they went on for weeks, sometimes even months.

I was exaggerating, of course; looking for excuses not to write, possibly. I seemed to be very good at that those days. Soon Jonas also started complaining: I came home and sat at the table to write, which meant that I expected to be served food. This complaint tasted like a well-known meal: in the years when Jonas had been completing his thesis, and I worked in a library, I had waited patiently for Saturday morning in order to write. Jonas had been very angry about this: he reasoned that he himself had been working all week on the thesis, and that he was looking forward to Saturday morning to do things with me. So if I wanted to write he would pick a fight. Then, as he noticed than when we fought I could not write for days, he would start picking fights on Friday evenings, just in case.

But that had happened a long time ago, when we were both very young. Now I saw that Jonas had a point. I was selfishly trying to finish my story, and was contributing to household chores less than ever. I was also angry by then, I was angry about the glove, of course. It was still there, lying on the floor, in exactly the same place where it had been tossed aside two weeks earlier.

I tried to explain that, if I came home and had to start collecting things from the floor or vacuuming, I had less time for my writing. This did not go down well, and Jonas went very serious and said that, until that moment, he had thought that I wanted to support his poetry, but that it was clear that I only wanted to have a servant, not a companion. He said that I behaved as if I wanted my pipe and slippers be brought to me by our trusty dog, that I expected to be waited upon. We did not have a dog, of course, they were so hard to come by. But I liked the image of this massive creature bringing my pipe and slippers to the table, as I sat down to try to finish my story. Some dogs in the past had rescued explorers and mountaineers from storms and blizzards. In order to do this, they carried casks of whisky hanging from their collars. These had to be massive, gigantic dogs, otherwise they could not carry casks of liquor. A dog of that size would probably not fit through the door of our little house. I knew that dogs came in all sort of sizes, they were one of the few mammals to have so much variety.

Anyway, Jonas said this and then opened the door and left. It was very late, almost one in the morning. I knew he would be gone all night, cycling in the dark and the cold. I also knew he was doing this to punish me. It was perfectly calculated: he knew I would be incapable of sleeping, and that the next day I would be exhausted. Still, I would drag myself to work and back. But at night I would be so tired that I would not be able to write anything. I would probably be so tired that, indeed, I would collapse on the sofa, needing to be waited upon, and that Jonas would do it willingly, even graciously. I would not be writing, and that would be punishment enough. Besides, he was ever the most charming of men the day after a fight, slickly attentive.

An American writer had kept peacocks, she called them the king of birds. The peacocks were very pretty, but also very proud, and she describes their behaviour in an essay she wrote, which makes them sound like they were birds that expected to be waited upon. She says they considered her a mere 'object' if she came to them without any food. If she had food, they would accept it. She also described their strutting beautifully, or rather the words were beautiful; but somehow I could not picture it. It was difficult picturing it from illustrations in books. I had been lucky enough to see a peacock feather once. It was kept in one of the colleges, one of its treasures. The college had been Jonas's father years ago, and he was still a member of sorts, so he got us in, one day, to see it. There was a big celebration going on and we got some lunch as well, nettle soup, sardine fritters, potato scones. The real thing as well, not made with fake potato puree. The feather was kept in the senior common room. It wasn't like I had expected. I had thought something spectacular would be revealed; but the feather looked lacklustre, dusty and void of life. It was also much smaller than

I had thought it would be. The dark blue oval on its tip made me think of an eye, made me think that the peacock was looking at me from the beyond. I felt faint and had to go out into the garden. It was then that I stumbled upon an unexpected conversation, Jonas's dad was talking about me with a colleague, describing my frequent questions about birds as 'idiotic'. Did this mean that I was idiotic, or that my questions were but I wasn't? Or was the package a complete thing? I could not make my mind up.

We left the college and went back home. I could not shake the disappointment the feather had caused me. In the olden days, there were programmes that recorded animals in their natural habitat. Apparently, they were made with the same machines that had made possible the fictitious series we watched on the television set. I had always wondered why they did not put them on television instead of the series. Jonas's father had told me once that they didn't schedule them on purpose, for the same reason that books with animals had been purged in the earlier days, and were so rare now. It was better if we all forgot about those things, healthier somehow.

3.

Many animals mated for life, according to my books and nature guides. Swans, and owls, and penguins, and albatrosses, and wolves, and eagles. Bittern, falcon, kestrel, heron, crow, sparrow. But not the kingfisher, it seemed. I read everything we had, everything I had managed to put together during nearly ten years. There was absolutely nothing there, nothing at all.

My dreams were getting more elaborate each night: the less I wrote the more I dreamed, apparently. I got some more reclaimed paper and cut each sheet in four pieces. Then I used my yarn needle and some left over yarn to tie it together. I put the little notebook on my bedside table with a pencil. The first night I had carefully prepared it all, sharpened the pencil, etc., nothing happened of course. But I left it there, just in case. Soon I started filling the notebook with ideas for short stories, impressions from my dreams, strange landscapes. If Jonas had read it he would have mocked me. But I knew somehow that I would understand the labyrinth of impressions when the time came to sit down and finally write.

I studiously avoided telling myself the truth: I was creating a list of possible stories that would never be written, little sentence-length cadavers, dead as soon as or even before I put them down on the page.

I was back there, back in the South. I was lying next to a little stream, which retched its muddy waters into a pool. I knew where I was immediately: it was a little forest on a hill next to the beach, overlooking the ocean. For some reason we had never ventured

172

there. I had never seen it, but in the dream I recognized it at once. I knew with the same certainty that the pond was the entrance to the virtual reality tunnel.

The dark rows of pine trees formed a canopy over my head. It was long since the pale pink flowers had blossomed on the almond trees, and the remaining buds released an acidic smell. I fell momentarily dizzy. The forest heaved with humidity; it was unbearably hot and sticky. Through the green ceiling I could catch glimpses of the sun, and little sparks of whiteness clouded my vision. I could hear the griffon vultures gliding above the trees, pungent shrieks, a disturbing, unnatural sound, which in the dream I recognized instantly. I was surrounded by plants and flowers: the stonecrop, the silver sage, the fragrant white virgin's bower. The blue and purple cliffhanger. Love-in-a-mist. Opium poppy. The hairy pink, the mournful widow. Beautiful, frightening, extravagantly unreal.

I could feel the heat inside my bones. The soaring temperatures indicated that soon all those flowers would die, in uncanny symmetry, one after the other. And then it would be summer.

We had not stayed so long down South, those months in August, September and October, when the temperatures get so high that it feels like hell on earth. Jonas had always said he did not want to be down there when it got really hot. Within the dream I understood something about the last fight in the apartment: Jonas had somehow manipulated the situation to get us back home. This made sense within the dream; as soon as I woke up I put the idea aside as too fanciful. But I also woke up to something else, a feeling of déjà vu. I remembered then that horrible time when I had had two part-time jobs, a library one, and the other one teaching Romance languages. I somehow got an interview for a university languages programme somewhere west. The teaching fellowship combined language instruction with PhD research, with fees paid by the department. A miraculous object, like a rare bird.

Jonas travelled with me to the interview in Cornwall. I had never travelled that far, and was surprised by how long it took us to get there: nearly two days with six changes. There was not much to do in the quaint little town, and the second-hand bookshops were not to Jonas's liking. He spent the whole trip sulking, obviously unhappy, and the long trip back speculating on how difficult it would be for him to live so far away from London. There were no academic libraries in the town, and he was turning his thesis into a monograph. He could not do it living so far away from an academic library, he explained. We simply could not afford his research trips. He did sums to demonstrate it. Train journeys were a luxury by then, the transport system an overcomplicated and dangerous thing. Hardly anyone could afford a car; it would be unimaginable that we could get one on my projected salary. Besides, they did not work so well in England, where sunlight was so scarce. Jonas would have to postpone writing the monograph, which might mean he would not get an academic job the following year. I did not dare to be responsible for that: he was the one with the doctorate after all, and our future pretty much depended on his being successful.

Perhaps things could have been different, but we were married by then. I am not sure exactly what that meant in my head, I could not put it into words. But it weighed a great deal somehow.

When we arrived back home, I got a phone call informing me that I had got one of the two fellowships on offer. The woman at the other end of the line could not believe it when I declined it. She shouted that no one had ever declined one of their fellowships before, and accused me of not knowing what I was doing. I found myself apologizing to her. Instead of going to Cornwall, we moved in with Jonas's parents. Jonas said we would be there for three months while he looked for a job. We ended up staying for almost a year.

And now we had somehow missed being down South for proper summer, when there would have been more chances to see the kingfisher. I had always wanted to experience that kind of heat: I had always imagined it would be full-blown, hellish summer, at the end of the world.

The bird lay twisted like a puppet by the roadside, unmoving. It was similar to and peculiarly different from the reproduction in the bird guides. The illustration, for starters, was not swarming with white worms. A red-and-yellow liquid covered the wound in its head, a watery mass of rotten flesh which had gushed over, melting into the muddy grass around it, making it impossible to know where the dead matter ended and the pine-coned ground began. For a second I imagined it was talking to me. Its voice sounded distant and strangely metallic, as though coming through a rusty pipe. Of course, there was no reason to imagine any of this. It was nonsensical. If the bird had wanted to communicate with me, it would not have talked, but rather chirped somehow. Why had I imagined its voice as a human voice?

There was an English writer who once thought that birds were talking to her, in Greek. She had written about women needing an income and a room of their own in order to write in peace. This was absurd: working in the library was providing me with an income, but there was hardly any time to do anything else. And there were many empty rooms in our house, as many as I could possibly want.

Jonas came by to see what I was staring at. He had seen me standing there from the kitchen window. He would tell me later that I looked so white, the grocery bags hanging from my limp arms, my long hair a tangled mess, he thought I was about to collapse on the floor. He commented in passing that a cat had probably got at the poor thing. A *cat*? What in earth did he mean? Everyone knew that there were no cats anywhere... Was it possible? I looked a Jonas, carelessly walking back into the house with the grocery bags he had taken from me. I fell a moment of void there and then, as it dawned on me, with the certainty of something that had been obvious for everyone else, but that for some reason you have not seen: Jonas was going mad.

There had been other signs, of course, but this casual comment about cats hunting birds topped it all.

I wanted to do something with the little thing. It seemed such a waste to bury him. But I could not stuffed it or preserve it in any way or form, that mass of liquid flesh and pulp and feathers. I went home and found an oak box we had been given for our marriage years back. I had never knew what to do with it, and now it had bits and pieces and lost keys. I emptied it by tipping all the contents over our bed. On the way out I took a plastic bag to use it as a glove to scoop the little bird, I placed it inside and left in by our shed. I knew that Jonas would not want it inside the house.

At least I had done something for now, although the time would come when I had to really decide what was to be done with it. But it didn't need to be now.

It came gradually, that realization of things not quite adding up. And then I noticed something odd, little grey fluffy things sometimes in Jonas's wake, like bits of fluff, although there were not fluff, exactly; they weren't feathers either, but I would say they sat in between these two things.

I started finding the little bits everywhere, but they seem to accumulate in two places in particular, the kitchen and the side of the sofa where Jonas sat in the evening to read his books, his little social media pager and his notebook always at hand, keeping me company while I watched television. He would stop reading when the pager beeped, take it, read something in it, and then he would have to get up and go to our old computer to post a reply, as his pager was a very old unbuttoned model. And the sofa cushion would then have the remains of I don't know what exactly; as if the promise of a grey bird had sat there instead of him. When Jonas came back, he always cleaned the little things with his hands in an uncaring way, as if he didn't see what they were, and mistakenly took them for actual fluff. How could he not see? His way of unseeing looked rehearsed to me, and I started doubting he didn't know what was going on. At night I lay next to him, dreading the moment when I would go to sleep.

My dreams had grown progressively more disordered, more untamed. The man in one had a red and puffed and sweaty face, but I could not see his features very well, and his eyes were two solid clumps of yellow dirt with two black seeds in the centre. His face was strangely close to mine, but what I could recognize were some trees, the jungle that I had explored in a previous dream, at the back of King's, close to the river. I could hear the parakeets, and I knew that they were the ones from our painted paper, back at home, loudly shrieking. Everything was getting mixed up, the way things do in dreams. His face blurred, his features faded away. Two eyes and a beak for a mouth. I could imagine myself somewhere else, not there. I could imagine I was the griffon vulture, looking at myself lying with the man on top of me. I then soared into the sky. I was flying, at last. But it wasn't the freeing sensation I had hoped for; instead, flying was heavy, so much effort, my limbs heavy and unmoving. I thought to myself that it was exactly like swimming, like swimming in the big bright sea; and I knew that the man had been right, the man in the plane, all those years ago. I had been too frightened, too angry, to believe him.

I sometimes thought that I had not forgiven Jonas for what happened with the fellowship, especially since he never finished his monograph, did not find a job. But there was also the question of money, and luck, and he could not be blamed for those. Back then Jonas had got a competent supervisor, which meant he had progressed smoothly in his studies, had managed to secure a grant. My experience was somehow different. My own supervisor had other interests at heart. It must have become clear to him very soon that nothing was going to happen. His reaction was not to see me at all, and I only managed a couple of supervisions during that whole academic year, such a crucial time when applying for grants.

For a long time I did not understand what was happening, why he had given up on me. In some ways I should be thankful, as it had been a miracle that I had left the programme both unscathed and with a master's degree.

Later on I learnt about his history, how he had kept a room on call in one of the most fancy hotels in town. I met him again sometime later. I was still in town, Jonas was finishing his thesis and I was, of course, working in a library. We coincided at a college dinner. I almost had a panic attack when I saw him. But that night he had decided to be genial. He went as far as apologizing, although he would not specify for what. The deed was not put into words. Until that night I had not fully realized the implications of what had happened, had not registered them, or had not wanted to. Still, he apologized. He was free of guilt now, whereas I would never recover the lost years, my failure to get a grant like Jonas had.

I became a bit of a wreck after that night, years after it had all happened. It was not surprising I had abandoned the possibility of the fellowship with the same ease with which I had said no to a paid librarianship degree. The truth was, I had no idea of what I wanted anymore, of how to exist within the world, of what the world wanted from me, where was I meant to go and what I was meant to do.

I woke up and Jonas was not there. Instead of him, a flurry of little feathers, grey, black, but also of other colours, brown and reddish and orange and white. I got worried that he would come back and find them there, and understand what was happening to him. So I collected them very carefully, all those little feathers, and put them in a plastic bag. Perhaps I could do something with them in the future, stuff a cushion or a pillow.

I looked through the window and then I saw it: his bike was nowhere to be seen. He had gone on one of his midnight cycles. But we hadn't had a fight, so I wasn't sure what the problem was. I went down to the kitchen and put the kettle on. I was resting against the counter, waiting for the kettle to boil, when I notice a stain in the middle of the room. It had little grey feathers, and they looked stuck to the floor somehow. There was an acidic, putrid smell. I found bleach and some old rags and cleaned it all. Some intuition told me that it would be better if Jonas did not see it, although at the same time I knew that the stain was connected to him, and that perhaps for that reason he had left the house. The feathers were in the middle of a gluey substance that reminded me to the liquid seeping out of the dead bird I had found. But it was something else, something indeterminate. I remembered the treatises on birds, how the deposits were explained. But if this was that, it must have been from a huge specimen.

I felt a strange desire to pick up the phone and call Jonas's dad for advice. But I could not do it. I could never ask him anything again. I was completely alone. I managed to clean everything up, and took out the old rags and everything I had used to the black rubbish bin, the one for unrecyclable materials. I went back in and had a shower. Then I boiled the kettle again, and this time sat in the sofa with a cup of tea, to wait for Jonas's return.

Jonas did not come back that morning, or the next night. Two days later I got back home from the library, and I saw his bike parked in our front garden. When I got in he was sitting in his usual place, reading, and greeted me as if he had only been away for ten minutes, not even bothering to look over the page.

I sat at the dining table, got my pen, looked through the pages of my unfinished story.

'Are you going to do that now?'

The words stabbed me a little, but I had no energy to react. I put the pen down, got up, sat next to him, and switched on the series rerun once more. We were getting to the end of the vampire killer one. The librarian did not feature any longer.

I realized that I had been angry with Jonas for years and years. But, somehow, I had got used to that as well, to being angry as such, and to existing within that anger. I had also been horrible to Jonas, for years and years. I had done cruel things to him.

That night I dreamt I was pregnant. But, instead of having a baby, I laid an egg. It looked like a dinosaur egg, purple and pinky, and full of ridged edges. It certainly did not look like any bird egg I knew from my pocket guide. The pocket guide was designed, as its name indicates, to go into your pocket. It belonged to a time when people were encouraged to go into nature and look for these wonders, and observe them in their natural habitat. You could find bird eggs everywhere it seems. The publication date was 1954, London.

I got up and sneaked out of bed. The whole room was full of little grey feathers, floating everywhere. They followed me while I came downstairs. They sat in the air gracefully, and danced in circles. I took a reading light that we had on a little table at the side of the sofa, and brought it to the dining table. I didn't want to risk the main light. I pushed the first sheet of paper inside the circle of light, took my pen, and started working on the story. I felt calm, strangely at peace. From time to time the house would crack and complain, and I would worry that it was Jonas, going to the toilet or similar. But it was never him, and I could continue working in the story uninterrupted. When the light changed and I knew it was time to get ready for work I had finished the first draft.

I could not believe it: it was finally done. A wave of relief came over me, as if I were playing dead in the middle of the ocean. Once, down the South, I had swum a bit too far. I had not realised how far away I was going. It was peaceful there, but I also panicked for a moment, when I saw that, however much I moved my arms and legs, I wasn't getting closer to the shore. Eventually I managed, with a superhuman effort. I would not die that day. But for a second the weight of the water and its embrace had been the most peaceful thing I had ever experienced.

After finishing the story things cleared up in my head. There were no strange dreams, or days when I would come to my senses in the library after a little fugue moment. Suddenly, all the feelings of paralysis left me. The world was filled with possibilities. I had energy to do anything I wanted. This was particularly absurd, since I had had to fight for each ounce of energy I possessed in order to finish the story.

As soon as I was done with a project, a little ritual ensued: I had to put away the papers and pencils and notes. This was a risky move: Jonas had been complaining that he could not finish anything these days. He had not written a poem in weeks. I didn't want to upset him. But having all the bits and pieces on the table, as if I still had work to do, created in me a strange anxiety. At least I did not need to worry about that at the moment. I had to go to the library. I had finally given in and collected the abandoned muddy glove, but we had had a huge fight about it, even fiercer than usual. At least now I could disappear into work, and not think about it for a few hours.

It was a very quiet day, one of those days outside term time when there are hardly any library users, and other jobs are finished behind the scenes. These jobs were always massive projects, hardly touched during the teaching terms, and therefore they got to us in those intervening weeks as huge and monstrous things. A couple of library assistants were helping me relocate a section of around five hundred books, tomes on and in a forgotten language that wasn't taught anymore in the faculty. We had discussed whether to weed that section entirely, keeping the most treasurable items in our Reserved Rooms. But I simply didn't have the heart to do it. I knew that weeding was a necessary thing in a small library like ours, more dedicated to teaching than to building a collection for future generations. That was the job of the main University Library. Purging meant that we could buy more things actually needed for the collection, instead of filling and overfilling space with items that the students didn't need. But I simply could not do it. I had managed to avoid it so far, I could not stand the idea of eliminating more things; but soon it would become apparent that it was my turn to kill something, seal its fate.

We managed to find a little unused corner where the forgotten language books would not be in anybody's way, and we left them there for the time being. Afterwards, I went up to see the finished job. An encyclopedia had been placed at the end of a bookshelf, and extended into the next one. Those two particular shelves were divided by a window. I bent down and retained in my head the last classmark, walked in front of the window towards the next bookshelf, intent on not forgetting what I had just seen, the little combination of letters and numbers, to check that the running number was correct. That must have been the reason why I hadn't looked directly into the window, why I had passed quickly in front of it. But the small shadow flicked in the corner of my eye, as the bird cleaned underneath his wing with his beak.

I took a step back and faced the window. And there it was, my kingfisher. There were no kingfishers in our river, there were no kingfishers in our town, there were probably none in the whole of England.

It was unmistakable, I knew it too well. Although my mind was resistant. My heart racing, I was trying to deny what my eyes were seeing. I reasoned with myself that it could be a bird from a close family. I reasoned it could be some kind of new hybrid. I reasoned that it could be a ghost. Then I saw what he was cleaning himself of: some little grey feathers. Or perhaps fluff. It didn't look at me, or noticed me staring at him. It simply took flight, so quickly and suddenly that I could not see where it went.

I got home later that day, no sight of Jonas. The house was a wreck, each and every one of the rooms a mess of grey feathers, blue feathers, pink feathers, gluey depositions, fleshy masses of indeterminate pulp. The furniture was covered in them, the walls in dark stains. The feathers floated everywhere. And the parakeets were speaking to me. They were loudly shrieking, like the griffon vulture back in the South, floating over the canopy of the forest, climbing up in the direction of the ocean. And they were telling me that he was not coming back, not coming back, not coming back.

4.

I scrubbed the house clean, the walls, the floors, the furniture. I phoned the library sick and spent a whole week cleaning, taking things out into the garden. Some of the furniture had been irrevocably lost, but it did not matter. Only one thing mattered: Jonas had not came back.

Winter had given way to Spring, and the library had filled with students and emptied once more, and once again filled up and emptied, as one term gave way to another. How curious it was that nearly all the towns where I had lived had large academic libraries at their centres, heaving like a living heart. And when they didn't, I felt a tiny bit lost. From the window of my office I could see the tower of the University Library, the beacon that guided us all. I looked at it from the distance, and caressed my rounded belly. It had happened like this: just as Jonas had left, my belly had started filling up. Everyone congratulated me, asked questions about the doctors, the nurses, all those people that I was meant to see, that were meant to see me. My answers were vague, rehearsed: I could not tell anyone the truth, that I had not been to see a doctor, because I did not want any doctor too look inside of me. I was sure that I wasn't carrying a child, but something else.

I was carrying an egg in my belly. It made perfect sense. When I circled it with my hands I could find no bumps, no kicks, but an even and hard curved thing, sitting underneath my flesh. Everyone insisted on my taking things easy, and tried to talk me into staying home, not coming to work. No one talked openly about the infertility epidemic, but they all repeated that I should not be coming. I guess they did not want a miscarriage in their midst. At the beginning I resisted the notion, but eventually I started staying at home two days a week, then four, then all the other days, as the delivery date approached. My belly grew and grew, so I guessed it might be a huge egg, like the one in my dream. Would my body be able to lay it? Or would the effort break me in two?

Now that I had all the time in the world I should have been writing, obviously. But things are never that simple. I went as far as bringing my 'dream' notebook into the dinning room, and preparing a little repository of reclaimed paper and sharpened pencils on the table. Every morning I made some coffee and sat there, reading through the notebook. I had been wrong thinking that I could interpret my notes. I could not understand what they where for, they seemed stupid, out of context, so utterly absurd. Jonas would have been right, of course. The truth was slowly dawning on me, a frightening thing that could not be ignored: I could not write. Jonas was not here, and that meant not knowing where he was, whether he was well or not. My mind heaved with the uncertainty. I could not concentrate on anything else.

Once, when I was young, I went through a time of sickness, when I was unable to write, by which I mean that I had actually, really, forgotten my own handwriting. When I noted down the titles of the few books I managed to read in my reading diary the letters were childish and uneven, unrecognizable. I still own that reading diary. Whenever I don't remember what it means to be sad I took it out and look at those pages.

The sickness lasted for a whole year. I could only explained it like this: one day I woke up and I had lost the will to live somehow. It was as if I were a solar battery from a car, and one day my energy levels went to minus zero, and for some reason I could not recharge them. I could not write, so instead I started gluing little pieces of coloured paper, magazines cut-outs, and even little objects, into a notebook.

A Spanish writer used to write novels and do collages. She was well-known for the novels, but no-one really knew about the collages very much. After she died they were published, and they threw so much light on the rest of her work, they should have been studied. But gluing little pieces of paper, knitting, sewing, and other domestic activities, have not traditionally mattered to anyone, mostly because only women did them in the olden days. Now all men are taught how to knit or sew, but only women can have babies. That is why no one is paying attention to the infertility epidemic, because it is thought of as a problem that belongs to us and us alone. The Spanish writer did many collages the year her only daughter died. Perhaps she couldn't write either, perhaps it seemed pointless to her, an idiotic activity, creating those fictitious worlds, those castles in the air made of words.

My own collages turned into monstrous things as soon as I incorporated the grey feathers that I had kept to make a cushion that night months ago, when it all started. In those first few days I had had to put away a great number of them. They took ages to be collected. I had tided them up inside plastics bags, and hid them in wardrobes all over the house. One day I got an idea. I looked through all the cupboards, and took out all the plastic bags with all the feathers. I found my yarn, and my sewing, I had no idea how I would do it, which medium or form it would take. The shirt would be made of feathers, to Jonas's measurements. It had to fit him properly, or he won't come back. I thought that, if I managed to achieve something as difficult as that, the universe would reward me with his return. The truth that I avoided telling myself was somehow different, of course: I needed something incredibly hard to accomplish, perhaps impossible, a project that would last days and weeks and months and years, to keep me from thinking about him.

So I set to work. I sewed all day and part of the night, watching my belly grow, like a rounded and hardened balloon, and in the early hours I fell asleep on the sofa to the lullaby of the parakeets shrieking that he was not coming back, not coming back, not coming back...

There was a town in the South filled with parakeets. They were not native to the local fauna, but the town had been an important port centuries back, and it was said that the first ones had escaped from a pirate's ship. They had propagated so quickly, so effectively they had contaminated the environment, that you could hear parakeets all day long, no matter where you were.

In the morning I woke up, made some coffee, went back to my work. It felt so utterly fiddly. The feathers would escape continuously, they danced around me, refused to be tamed. As I did my job, my belly continued growing, until one day it seemed to have grown enough. I could not move from the sofa anymore; I was a rounded thing. I had stopped eating and drinking, and I only counted feathers. That titanic effort; the more feathers I put where I wanted, more feathers seemed to be lying in the floor, floating in the air, dancing ironically around me. I needed to rest, but the rest of someone who had undertaken an enormous effort: built a castle in one day, turned a barn-full of wheat into gold, drained a lake. And I didn't have anyone to help me. I was completely alone.

I think that I had called upon the kingfisher myself, I was so lonely. One night something broke inside me, and I felt as if all the water in the world would fall from me. I got up awkwardly, opening my legs, and tried to make it to the kitchen. In the landing of the house I bent and fell on my knees. Something told me to go on my fours and push and push. I think I saw him then, the kingfisher, looking at me from the entrance cabinet.

I pushed and pushed and pushed once more, but whatever was coming seemed huge, impossible. It did feel as if I was in fact breaking; but I didn't, of course.

When it was all over I was shocked to see what had come out of my body. Two legs, two arms, one perfect little head, blue and red and gluey. And Jonas's eyes, of course. I sat there, panting, in disbelief. It took all my will to go to the little thing and take her in my arms. She was crying, shouting perhaps, and I could make up some words behind the shrieking: he is here, he is here, he is here. The parakeets were silent.

A Place for Wild Beasts

Nina was sure she knew what the problem was. She had an instinct for this kind of thing; a translator, perhaps, but she came from a long line of Norfolk farmers. She went out to inspect her precious cherry tomatoes. The big pot didn't like the wall it was leaning against, that was all. It would be difficult to move it on her own, but she would manage. Better get it done.

'What the...?'

The tulips had gone.

If she was going to learn something in the next few days, was the systematic way with which the deer applied itself to eat each and every one of the flowers in her garden. It was as if it had a preconceived plan of sorts, or followed some kind of logic. It had appeared to favour yellow flowers, for example. Then purple. Then pink. Now it was munching the lot.

Hedgehogs, rodents, foxes. Every imaginable kind of English garden bird. What she had not expected at all was a deer so near the city centre.

There could be no possible confusion. The little camera had revealed the creature in all its antlered glory. During the days that she endured the peculiar invasion, she kept repeating to herself that that night she would get up and shoo it away. But she had never managed to wake up for some reason, and had always looked at the images the next day, transfixed, of course. How else?

Seriously, what was a deer doing in *her* garden?

One night she decided not to go to sleep. The garden was by now a desolate patch of green mould, with the stems of the flowers moving with the wind. But she knew it would still come. It seemed that it had some kind of fixation, and there were still some late roses languishing in a corner it had not yet got to. Nina drank coffee right after dinner. She sat on the couch, with the laptop on the coffee table, inspecting eagle-eyed the dark scene on the screen. Despite all her preparations, she fell asleep, and the next morning she found the kitchen door to the garden open, and muddy hoofmarks ran up and down the kitchen floor. There must have been at least three or four deer there. Either that, or her own deer—for she now thought of the deer as her own, with a certain proprietary sense—had been very active. As active as to cross that last red line. This was unacceptable. She would have to do something that very night. Besides, how was it possible she had heard nothing?

'This is utterly ridiculous!'

She had a nap in the middle of the afternoon, something she had never done before. It was difficult to go to sleep. But she woke up refreshed, when dark was falling. She had slept more than she had intended to.

At the right time she was awake, inspecting the screen. There it was. Where was he heading this time?

She went into the kitchen, and opened the garden door as slowly as possible. She did not want to scare it with any noise, she wanted to shoo it away personally, to get rid of it herself. She felt this was important, to mark her territory. Go away! Eat someone else's flowers!

So she went into the garden and there it was.

Such a beautiful creature, as stunning and dignified as a king.

'Oh, I see,' she murmured. To the deer, perhaps to herself.

Nina went back into the house, and started packing straight away. The next morning a taxi pulled up at her door, and she left her house forever. It was the right thing to do.

Q&A with Timothy J. Jarvis

Q. The more pressing climate change has become, the more fiction has concerned itself with ecological collapse, and the last few years has seen an explosion of novels and story collections which explore environmental crises. Much of this is aftermath fiction. The trope of 'plucky' survivors on some kind of pilgrimage through a desolated world, driven by urges and whims opaque even to them, has now become almost rote. It seems to me that the stories in Lost Objects *take a very different approach, climatic change depicted not as dramatic upheaval, but slow creep. In 'Kingfisher' there is even a question mark hanging over what precisely is being experienced. And even in the post-crisis tales, like 'The Ravisher, The Thief', the worlds feel less blasted, more convincing (maybe even more hopeful, though absolutely not glibly so). How did you go about developing this unique way of writing imaginatively about loss and decay?*

A. Part of the problem with climate change is that it's difficult for us to even acknowledge it: this is a clear 'slow-creep' wicked problem. As a writer I want to address this distantiation that we experience. I personally am a writer of liminality, rather than certainties. Perhaps this is connected with being a bit of an outsider: I look at English society from the margins, never fully included, so I myself am used to inhabiting these liminal spaces. Understandably, this has seeped into my writing, grounding it firmly in the 'not-quite-there'. My main interest is in exploring these liminal moments, these grey areas, unsure spaces where boundaries blur and nothing is too clean-cut. Most of my fiction deals with these places, one way or another.

Q. One other feature of much contemporary climate fiction is that it is generally tied to human characters and an anthropocentric perspective. Your stories seem to approach change on a more universal scale and distribute consciousness to the non-human—animal and even insentient (the curious malevolence of the alien world in 'Frozen Planet'). Was this a conscious choice? What lay behind it? How was it done?

A. All writing is political, right? All art is political. I certainly think that human beings + capitalism are to blame for this mess. I know this may sound a simplistic answer, but we, majorly, are the agents of chaos. I like giving non-human creatures agency in my stories, whether is a garden or a farm that reconquers space, a deer that throws a woman out of her own house, even a massive digital library in my story 'Player/Creator/Emissary'—an idea that I anticipated in my novel *The Swimmers*—all of them have something in common: they are fighting us, quite clearly. I am reframing the human as the main villain here. Perhaps I am also manifesting the kind of world that I would like to pass through? I think humanity's time has passed, and we are not even aware of this.

Q. A simple question—why birds? Birds are key to so many of the tales—and in 'Kingfisher' the eponymous bird becomes totem and then catalyst—the protagonist's husband dissolves into downy feathers of many hues, and she becomes miraculously pregnant. There is also a strand in that story about writers' relationships to birds, Milton's in the epigraph, and both O'Connor's peacocks and Woolf's Greek-talking birds are alluded to. What is your own relationship to birds?

A. Birds are beautiful, they are liminal creatures: birds move between realms. There is a song by Lisa O'Neill that I am obsessed with: 'Birdy from another realm', where she explains how in the presence of birds we are in the presence of something entirely otherworldly. Then there is their connection with something that truly fascinates me as much as it terrifies me: the idea of 'deep time'. A bird is our closest connection, and in fact a direct one, with the dinosaurs. How incredible is that? I am obsessed with things that connect us with deep time. My partner gave me a Burmese amber ring recently: it is meant to be about 86 million years old. I cannot even start to imagine the concept of having something that existed then on top of my finger. We are so truly insubstantial. Throughout our lives, we become trapped, at times in cages of our own making. And it's so hard to understand this while it's happening. Birds encompass all of this at once: the idea of freedom, but of freedom to escape our world by moving between worlds, between different epochs even, the now and the then... And birds will be here long after we have gone. They are my metaphor for everything that we are not.

Q. Linguistic play and transmutation is at the heart of many of these stories. The protagonists of 'Kingfisher,' 'A place for wild beasts,' and 'The Ravisher, The Thief' are translators and a buried etymology is key to understanding the latter tale. How has your own work as a translator and your ability to move fluidly between languages fed into your writing?

A. Have you watched *Only Lovers Left Alive*? It's one of my favourite movies. There is a scene when Tilda Swinton is packing to go and visit her lover, played by Tom Hiddleston, and she is not packing clothes, but books, in every language imaginable... Every time I see that scene, I completely relate: if I was immortal, and had all the time in the world at my disposal—Swinton is playing a vampire—I would definitely do two things: learn languages and learn to play instruments. I love the idea of reading what I want, of watching the movies I want, of travelling anywhere and being able to speak with anyone I meet.

I am aware that writing in a 'chosen' language is a privilege; but bilingualism, and even multi-linguality, must be celebrated: they allow you to understand somebody else in their own terms, which is outstanding. I am fascinated by this idea of understanding one another, of translation and language as a means of building bridges. Again, this is a political action, even if it sprouts from the act of writing, you are creating a different version of something, with the intention of expanding its reach. Translation can also be ideologically motivated, so as a tool we need to use it with care, be respectful, be aware of what we are doing. I hope that these small ideological actions are what are left in my writing. I write in order to understand the world, I also write in order to explain it, and to offer others the chance to reflect upon it. The possibility of doing so in more than one language, if you can, needs to be taken.

There's also a more personal reason here: as much as a bridge, moving between languages can be used as a shield: I feel freer to experiment writing in English, to try things out, and to explore possibilities, in a way that writing in Spanish would not allow me to. Spanish for me is the language of growing up with Catholicism being pushed down your throat, or female oppression, in the household, but also outside of domestic spaces, openly, violently.

Q. Lastly, can you summarise your personal aesthetic as a writer?

A. When I published one of my first stories written in English, 'Orange Dogs', in *Weird Fiction Review*, the magazine had the kindness to interview me. I was asked to describe my personal aesthetic then. I hadn't given this much thought, but three words came to mind at once, and they've guided me ever since: Beauty is complicated. I think that simply sentence comprises a lot about what I think about writing, about art. There is beauty in desolation, as much as there is despair in perfection. Everything needs darkness and light to become real. Our world is extremely polarised, and, as I explained above, I understand better the spaces in-between those dichotomies. I am a explorer of the liminal, and my writing wants to become a door to that. I hope some of it manages it.

TIMOTHY J. JARVIS is a writer with an interest in the antic, the Weird, and the strange. His cult 'last man' novel The Wanderer *was first released in 2014 and republished in 2022, and his supernatural short tales are collected in* Treatises on Dust, *currently longlisted for the Edge Hill Prize. He lives in Bedford, a small town in the hallowed/ cursed M1 corridor.*

ACKNOWLEDGEMENTS

Thank you to Francesca Tristan Barbini and Luna Press Publishing for publishing the first edition of this collection in 2018. Thank you to everyone who reviewed and helped spread the word about it: *The Fantasy Hive*, *Los Angeles Review of Books*, *Interzone*, *Black Static*, *Runalong the Shelves*, *Weird Fiction Review*, *Vol. 1 Brooklyn*, *Yale Climate Connections* etc.

Thank you to the friends who support my writing and keep me going, and to all the many admired writers who endorsed this book: Nina Allan, Priya Sharma, Helen Marshall, Jonathan Thornton, Sofia Rhei, Jasmine Kirkbride, Vida Cruz, Martin Cahill, Jeff VanderMeer, Gary Budden, Una McCormack, Elizabeth Hand, Tim Major, Timothy J. Jarvis, Liliana Carstea.

Thank you to Priya and Tim for the introduction and the questions. Thank you to James for his editorial wizardry. Thank you to Vince Haig for designing a beautiful cover for this book, twice. Thank you to you, reader, for reading this book.

CAMBRIDGE, HALLOWE'EN 2024

This edition of *Lost Objects*
was sent to print
on 14 October 2024,
anniversary of the birth in 1888
of the writer Katherine Mansfield

CALQUE PRESS